HIDDEN LAUGHTER

Also by Simon Gray

# HIDDEN LAUGHTER

## Simon Gray

*faber and faber*

LONDON · BOSTON

First published in 1990
by Faber and Faber Limited
3 Queen Square London WC1N 3AU
Reprinted 1991

Photoset by Wilmaset Birkenhead Wirral
Printed in England by Clays Ltd, St Ives plc

A CIP record for this book is
available from the British Library

ISBN 0–571–14433–0

For Sarah

Sudden in a shaft of sunlight
Even while the dust moves
There rises the hidden laughter
Of children in the foliage
Quick now, here, now, always –
Ridiculous the waste sad time
Stretching before and after.

*from* 'Burnt Norton', T. S. Eliot

*Hidden Laughter* was first presented by Michael Codron on 12 June 1990 at the Vaudeville Theatre, London. The cast was as follows:

| | |
|---|---|
| HARRY | Kevin McNally |
| LOUISE | Felicity Kendal |
| BEN | Richard Vernon |
| RONNIE | Peter Barkworth |
| DRAYCOTT | Sam Dastor |
| NATALIE | Caroline Harker |
| NIGEL | Samuel West |
| NAOMI | Jane Galloway |
| | |
| *Lighting Designer* | Rick Fisher |
| *Set Designer* | Robin Don |
| *Directed by* | Simon Gray |

# ACT ONE

## SCENE ONE

*Evening. Country cottage. Only the garden is visible. It is twilight.* LOUISE *and* HARRY *come out from the house into the garden. They stand for a moment, staring. The garden is well kept, but there is an anomalous tree stump in its centre.*

HARRY: I say!

LOUISE: It's beautiful. Beautiful. Just as I've always imagined. (*They walk forward.*) And so lovingly looked after. Look at the roses. They've been pruned.

HARRY: And the grass cut. You could bounce a ball along it. Strange – didn't the chap in the estate agents say it belongs to an old lady they've put into a home – yes, here it is (*Looking at particulars*) Ivy Cottage. Great Yarcombe. I've made a note. Owner ga-ga.

LOUISE: She must be, from the state of the house. I've never seen anything so . . . so desolate. And the smell!

HARRY: But the fact is, darling, it's just the right size. Rooms for each of the children. The living room, the kitchen and a sort of dining area we can make out of the scullery, our room, and the room at the back for Daddy.

LOUISE: Isn't it a bit small? I mean, if he's going to be putting up half the money –

HARRY: Yes, well, we'll let him choose. Obviously we'd have to have the large bedroom as there are two of us – and we'd want the children in rooms next to ours –

LOUISE: Well, that really only leaves that room. So he can't really choose –

HARRY: Well, talk it over, I meant. I'm sure he'll be perfectly pleased with that one – he's so keen on our getting somewhere.

LOUISE: We'd have to come down every weekend. For it to make sense.

HARRY: Well, we'll certainly try to. Otherwise what would be the point? It's a big step. Even with Daddy's half.

I

LOUISE: Darling, are you absolutely sure we can afford it?

HARRY: No, we can't really. But have faith, my love. We'll manage.

LOUISE: Oh, I do have faith. In you, anyway. And if anything goes wrong we can always sell . . .

HARRY: Exactly! House prices are bound to go up and up, especially in this little corner of Devon. So –

LOUISE: So. I think . . . if it hadn't been for this – (*Looking around*) this little acre of paradise –

HARRY: A quarter of an acre. (*Checking particulars.*)

LOUISE: I'd have thought we were mad. But I feel . . . feel it's claiming us. As if it's been keeping itself trim and beautiful and friendly especially for us. Only for us.

HARRY: I know what you mean.

LOUISE: (*Shyly*) Another thing.

HARRY: What?

LOUISE: I think I could write here.

HARRY: Write? Write what?

LOUISE: Well, I don't know. Stories – novels even, I thought.

HARRY: Ah.

LOUISE: Don't you want me to?

HARRY: Yes, yes, of course I do, darling.

LOUISE: That fragment I showed you, you were so encouraging.

HARRY: What fragment?

LOUISE: Before we were married.

HARRY: Oh yes, I'm sorry, darling. I've seen so many fragments from so many writers since – the autobiographical piece.

LOUISE: You said it showed I had it in me to be a real writer, why didn't I go the whole hog and aim for a book.

HARRY: Well darling, if that's what you really feel you want to do – instead of going back to teaching, wasn't that the plan, when the children – ?

LOUISE: It's just the feeling I get here. In this garden. This evening. A sense of . . . of a future.

HARRY: So –
LOUISE: So –
HARRY: I make an offer, then.
LOUISE: Oh yes. Oh yes please.
    (*They embrace.*
    BEN *enters, from the garden side and stands watching them.*)
HARRY: (*Sees him*) Oh, Daddy! – well, we think this could be
    the one.
LOUISE: *Is* the one, Ben.
HARRY: What do you say?
BEN: (*Looks around, rather blankly*) Really? Well, yes – I
    suppose with a bit of work . . . Saw a rat inside – big
    brute of a fellow – just trudged past me. Nasty smells
    everywhere too – damp rot, holes in the roof –
LOUISE: Oh, we know all about that, Ben.
HARRY: We'll clear out the rats, Daddy, and the damp, don't
    worry.
LOUISE: And look at this, Ben. This is the point. (*Gestures
    around.*) You see?
    (BEN *stares around, not quite understanding.*)
HARRY: Isn't it the most lovely garden!
BEN: Oh. Oh yes. Yes. (*Peering*) Hollyhocks, aren't they?
    (*Turns away, his shoulders shaking.*)
    (LOUISE *and* HARRY *exchange a look.*)
LOUISE: Oh, Ben. (*Goes over, puts her arms around him.*)
HARRY: Daddy. (*Goes to him uncertainly, puts a hand on his
    shoulder.*)
BEN: Sorry. Sorry. (*Wiping eyes*) Don't know where it comes
    from. Just leaps up when I'm least expecting it.
    (*Attempts to stifle sob.*) Wells up. Inside me. Like a
    lump –
HARRY: It's all right, Daddy. It's all right. You can cry or
    scream or shout – anything you want – with us.
LOUISE: Yes, Ben. It's nothing to be ashamed of. Grief.
BEN: (*Attempting to compose himself*) Well, nothing . . .
    nothing in my experience, I suppose. Prepared me for it.
    Couldn't imagine a life without her, you see. Forty

years. Most of my whole life, adult life. And of course I keep thinking that in some way it was my fault, if I'd taken better care of her –

HARRY: You were a wonderful husband, Daddy.

BEN: Was I? Was I? How do I know whether I was? I was her only husband, perhaps some other man . . . some other man –

HARRY: There couldn't have been another man, Daddy. You and she –

LOUISE: She was always telling me about her luck in the two men she had in her life.

BEN: Two men? Two? What do you mean, two?

HARRY: I think she meant me, Daddy.

LOUISE: Of course she meant you.

HARRY: Yes, of course she did. Sorry. I was just using 'think' as a figure of speech. She meant me, Daddy. You and me.

BEN: (*Stands bewildered*) What do I do now? What do I do now?

(HARRY *looks at* LOUISE.)

LOUISE: You make a new life, Ben.

HARRY: And we're here, Daddy. You're surrounded by love and support. And there'll be this house – so much to do to get it just right.

BEN: But it seems so unfair – she always wanted us to settle in the country, but I wouldn't, said we couldn't afford it, but now of course, with the insurance money and –
(*Stands, shoulders shaking, sobbing helplessly.*)
(RONNIE *enters through the garden, in dog collar, etc.*)

RONNIE: Um, hello – I do hope you don't mind – I was passing and heard voices – I'm, um, Ronald Chambers, the . . . the local – (*Taking in scene*) I'm so sorry. I'm intruding. (*Makes to go.*)

HARRY: No, no, we were just . . . just admiring the garden.

BEN: I've a touch of hay-fever, 'fraid. (*Blowing his nose.*) Must be the hollyhocks.

RONNIE: Hollyhocks? Oh, the geraniums –

4

BEN: Or the roses. They always get right up my nose. (*Laughs.*)

LOUISE: We were wondering who'd kept the garden up – we'd understood that the old lady who owned the house was rather frail.

RONNIE: Yes, well actually not frail, old May was as strong as an . . . an ox in some ways. But a bit, um – you see. Especially these last few years. But she kept at the garden – in fact she was actually going at it with her trowel when they came to take her away two months ago. (*Little pause. Blinks vaguely.*) Does that answer your question?

LOUISE: Oh, how . . . how touching.

HARRY: Well, it doesn't really. That is, if you take the question as being – who's kept it up since.

RONNIE: Oh, of course, yes, that was the question, wasn't it? Yes. Well, I suppose the answer has to be, well, me. Yes. In as much as I've been coming in a few times a week, an hour or so an afternoon here, an afternoon there, just when I had a minute or two – to keep it up. Sometimes I've even had a bash at the tree stump – couldn't shift it though, not by an inch, and so I decided old May really wants it where it is. Are you interested?

LOUISE: Oh yes, please go on.

RONNIE: No, I meant in . . . in purchasing. I take it you're looking around with a view to . . . purchasing?

LOUISE: Well, the truth is, we've made up our minds. We're going to make an offer. Aren't we, darling?

HARRY: We're going further than that, darling. We're going to buy. Aren't we, Daddy?

BEN: We bloody well are! Oh sorry, forgive my language.

HARRY: (*Laughing*) My father was in the Diplomatic, you see.

BEN: Well, not really the Diplomatic – Ministry of Trade, but bit of a troubleshooter all over the globe. Left footprints from Peru to Portugal, eh, Harry? (*Laughs.*)

(RONNIE, HARRY, LOUISE *join in laughter, slightly awkwardly*.)

RONNIE: (*To* HARRY) May I, um, may I ask – what line *you're* in?

HARRY: An agent.

RONNIE: Ah. An agent.

HARRY: A literary agent.

RONNIE: Really! A literary – I hadn't thought of Great Yarcombe as a place for a literary agent to . . . to set up shop, so to speak, but of course with the telephone and so forth, why ever not?

LOUISE: Actually we're not going to have a telephone. That's one thing we've absolutely promised ourselves, haven't we, darling? When we're here we want to be completely cut off. Nothing and nobody from London.

RONNIE: Oh, I see. It's a weekend cottage you're . . . you're –

LOUISE: I expect you disapprove.

BEN: Disapprove, Lou! Why should he disapprove?

HARRY: Well, Daddy, you know – Londoners taking over housing when locals, natives, I mean the people who were born and bred here – we push the prices up, you see.

RONNIE: Nobody around here wants this house, I do assure you. Nobody at all. Most of the young people want to move to London. Or Salisbury, at the least. Have you any . . . any, um, children?

LOUISE: We have indeed.

HARRY: Two. A boy and a girl.

BEN: Nig and Nat they're called, Reverend, a couple of mischievous charmers, never know what they're up to from one moment to the next . . .

RONNIE: How delightful, how delightful, and how old are they – did you say?

BEN: Nat is nine and Nig is eight.

HARRY: Nearly right, Daddy, except it's the other way around.

6

LOUISE: (*Hitting names emphatically*) *Nigel* is eight and *Natalie* is nine.

HARRY: No, darling, the other way around again. Natalie is eight and Nigel is nine.

RONNIE: Lovely age, whichever way around it is, and so I suppose you left them in London, did you, while you . . . you – (*Gestures.*)

HARRY: No, no, we brought them down. They're here. At least I hope they are. (*With a little laugh.*) They are still in the car, aren't they, Daddy?

BEN: Yes, yes. Well no, actually, I let them out into the field.

LOUISE: The field?

BEN: Well, there's not much they can get up to in a field, Lou, is there, Fa – Reverend?

RONNIE: Oh, do call me Ronnie. Please.

HARRY: Ronnie. Harry Pertwee. Louise (*Indicating*) and my father.

BEN: Ben. Ben Pertwee.

(*They nod and smile at each other.*)

RONNIE: (*To* BEN) Which field did you leave them in exactly, um?

BEN: Oh, the big one just up the road, to the left.

RONNIE: (*Looks worried*) Ah. That'd be old Tomalin's, I expect. A rather . . . rather ferocious old character.

LOUISE: You mean he may not like our two being in his field.

RONNIE: Oh, no, I'm sure, quite sure – when it comes to it – two young lives – he'll take a bit of care with the heifers. And old Dan.

BEN: Old Dan?

RONNIE: Yes, that's the, um, that's the bull. He lets them in (*Checks his watch*) about now. He likes to use that field, you see, because it blocks the way to Great Yarcombe, the public footpath. Old Tomalin! (*Shakes his head.*) But really his bark's far worse than his bite.

HARRY: And what about the bull? Is his bark worse than his bite?

RONNIE: Oh, he's got a bit of a reputation, you know, but I've never heard of any really serious, um –

LOUISE: Darling, I really think we'd better get up there.

HARRY: Yes, we had. (*Moving towards back.*)

RONNIE: Actually it'll be quicker if you go by the gate, the little path takes you straight to it.

HARRY: Oh, right.

LOUISE: (*Following*) I do wish you hadn't left them alone, Ben.

(LOUISE *and* HARRY *hurry off. There is a pause.*)

RONNIE: I wonder if I should go with them. As I know the terrain, so to speak.

BEN: No, don't worry, no need for a hue and cry. To tell you the truth, old Lou's a charming girl, dead right for Harry, but she's a slight tendency to fuss and fret. Anyway, where the children are concerned. Where most things are concerned. I'm always trying to get her to take a leaf from my Emily's book.

RONNIE: Emily's your, um – your, um –

BEN: Widow. I mean, my wife. Dead wife. I'm a widower, is how I intended to put it. Died four months ago. My wife, that is. Emily.

RONNIE: I'm very sorry.

BEN: Don't be! Don't be! I'm not. She had a good life. And a . . . a . . . it was very quick. Mercifully quick. Her death, I mean. God though, I miss her.

RONNIE: Yes, I'm sure you do.

BEN: Nothing's the same. Nothing's the same without her. I mean, there we were in our little house in Kingston, years still ahead of us so we thought. Good years. Retirement years. And suddenly . . . suddenly I find myself all alone in some little service flat in Fulham – oh, perfectly nice place, perfectly convenient – Harry and Louise found it for me – but still I find myself thinking what am I doing here without Emily, how's it happened? How? (*Nearly breaks down again, manages to control himself.*) And you? You married?

8

RONNIE: Yes. Yes, I am. Well, in the sense that I have a – have a wife. If you follow. But she . . . she . . .

BEN: Left you?

RONNIE: Oh, no. No. Not that. No. But she's not . . . not altogether – she's been ill on and off for quite a few years. Since the year after we got married, in fact. She spends a lot of the time in a . . . a . . .

BEN: Wheelchair?

RONNIE: No, no, not that sort of illness. In a home. So to speak. Mentally ill, you see.

BEN: Oh. Oh dear. I'm sorry.

RONNIE: No, no, don't be. Some of the time she's very happy. In fact, a surprising amount of the time. Well, it's a private home, you see, um, um – her name's Wilemena.

BEN: Must be difficult. Even in your position.

RONNIE: No, no. An exceptionally nice woman comes in from the village, looks after me – Mrs Mossop. A widow herself – in her fifties – well, she was when she started. So in her sixties now, come to think of it. Cleans the vicarage, cooks my meals, does my laundry . . .

BEN: No, I mean believing in God. Hard to believe in a God who condones madness, death . . .

RONNIE: Oh, quite. Almost impossible.

BEN: I have to tell you, been a lifelong atheist. Fervent.

RONNIE: Oh, I . . . I don't blame you. Quite understand. Most of my parishioners are like that. Don't believe a word of it. Don't listen to a word of it. Usual . . . usual Christians, these days in England. Christmas day, Easter, weddings and funerals.

BEN: I'm sorry. I mean, from *your* point of view.

RONNIE: Oh, not at all. I fully understand, appreciate their points of view. And really the whole thing is so . . . so preposterous, isn't it? In this day and age.

BEN: (*Angrily*) You mean you don't believe in God!

RONNIE: Well, well, I wouldn't put it quite like that, Dan.

BEN: Ben.

9

RONNIE: Mmm? Oh yes, sorry. Ben.

BEN: Dan's the old bull.

RONNIE: Mmmm? Oh – oh, (*Laughs*) so he is, the murderous old monster.

BEN: Well, do you or don't you believe in God?

RONNIE: I don't know – well, who can say – but . . . but . . . the point is – you see, there's no point in believing in him unless it's impossible to believe in him, if you follow, because if he existed, and we all knew he existed there'd be no difficulty at all in believing in him and what'd be the point in *that*. (*Little pause*) I've put that rather badly, Dan, Ben, all I mean is that faith is . . . is a matter of believing what's impossible to believe. Do you, um, see? Otherwise it's not faith. It's certainty. If you follow.

BEN: The certainty's all I've got to believe in. The certainty that this impossible bloke of yours, that you call God, allows people like my Emily and your, your, your – (*Gestures*.)

RONNIE: Wilemena.

BEN: To go mad. To die. So I'd prefer it if he wasn't there to be responsible for it. Otherwise all there is to believe in is a nasty piece of work.

RONNIE: But . . . but if he does exist, impossible though it may be to believe, then whatever he's up to would be impossible to understand. That's all I . . . I – that's my whole – the mystery of it. If there is a mystery. If it turns out that there isn't, then you're right, of course, Ben.

BEN: But for God's sakes, how can you – how dare you – if that's as far as you can go, how do you expect the rest of us, me, for instance, if *nobody*, including types like you who are paid for it – I mean, it's your bloody job to believe in God, damn it! If you don't, who will?

RONNIE: I know, I know. But we do try, you see, and quite a few of the other chaps actually manage it, I suppose. Really do believe in him on a day to day basis. And the rest of us – those of us who find it impossible, well, we just have to make the leap – the leap into the (*Gestures*) dark!

(LOUISE *appears at the gate, clearly distraught.*)

LOUISE: (*To* RONNIE, *urgently but attempting control*) Could you please come and have a word with that horrible old farmer? He won't let my husband in to look for the children, just swears and shakes his stick and threatens to set the bull on us – and they could be . . . could be trampled to death for all he cares!

RONNIE: (*As he goes towards gate*) Oh, I'm sure even old Tomalin –

LOUISE: (*Suddenly panic-stricken*) Oh, please hurry, please, please! (*As she moves off.*)

BEN: What? What's happening? (*Pause, then he makes uncertainly to go after* RONNIE *and* LOUISE. *There is the sudden laughter of children from two different parts of the garden, off.*) What?

### SCENE TWO

*Three years later. Late afternoon. Full sunshine. The inside of the house is now visible. A small sitting room, with a minimum of furniture – a large table, a door stage right, that leads to stairs up to the bedrooms. A door, stage left, that leads to a short hall (not visible on stage) that leads to a kitchen, not yet fully equipped, but with an oven, a fridge, table and chairs.*

LOUISE *is sitting at the table, typing with minimum fingers but with great speed and controlled energy.*

HARRY *is in the garden, in which there is now a swing. He is digging with controlled energy at the unsightly stump.*

*Louise's typing accelerates to a kind of climax.*

HARRY *accelerates his digging, almost as if in time to the typing, to a point of demented ferocity.*

LOUISE *concludes a sentence with an appropriate flourish, sits staring at the page in triumph.*

HARRY *glances towards* LOUISE, *as if unconsciously aware that the typing has stopped, then throws down his spade and starts to grapple with the stump, swaying and levering it this way and that.*

LOUISE *gets up, stretches happily, goes off left, appears in the kitchen, peers into the oven, then takes a bottle of white wine out of the fridge, a corkscrew, and three glasses.*

HARRY, *meanwhile, continues to grapple with the stump, swearing at it, almost* sotto voce *initially, but his swearing getting louder and louder.*

HARRY: Come on, you sod, come on, you bastard, come on, come on, oh, you brute – you swine – you . . . you . . . (*Reels back, having lost his footing, then lurches forward again, as if about to assault a human enemy.*) You . . . you shit! (*Grapples with it briefly, then gives up.*)
(LOUISE *comes out with tray.*)

LOUISE: Oh, isn't this heaven!

HARRY: Mmmm?

LOUISE: It's always at its best at this time of the evening. Really, as if it were a blessed spot. I sometimes believe the sun isn't shining anywhere else in the world – at least, with that special softness. (*Puts tray down.*) What have you been doing?

HARRY: Oh, I just thought I'd have a go at the stump. (*Sits on swing.*) I'll have another go tomorrow, before we leave. Half an hour should do it.

LOUISE: Odd. You know I've got rather fond of him. I mean he's always been here –

HARRY: No, he hasn't always been here, darling. Any more than we have. And it's time he went. Him or me.
(LOUISE *strokes his hair, then kisses him on the back of the neck.*)

LOUISE: Oh, you're so hot.

HARRY: Am I? (*Catches her hand, kisses the back of it.*)

LOUISE: And you smell.

HARRY: Yes, I expect I do.

LOUISE: No, but it's delicious. Manly. Lovely and manly. I could gobble you up.

HARRY: Why don't you then? (*Sinking to the grass.*) The house is empty. We're ocompletely private. I'm reasonably available.

LOUISE: (*Comes over to him, licks at his face*) We won't be private in a few minutes. Go on (*Draws him to his feet*) open the wine.

HARRY: (*Seeing three glasses*) Oh, Ronnie, of course. I wonder what he did before we came. Or does while we're not here. Which is most of the time. (*Begins to open bottle.*)

LOUISE: Well, one of the things he does is keep our garden up for us – and he's done it beautifully. So do say something nice and grateful to him, darling.

HARRY: Yes, yes, he's been a real trump. You know, I agree with you. (*Looking around, almost as if for first time.*) It does feel a blessed place. I suppose because the house seems really ours at last, as if we've a real stake in it, invested part of ourselves.

LOUISE: It does seem a bit treacherous, though. I mean, to have come without Nigel and Natalie.

HARRY: That's because we've never done it before. But we'll do it again. A trial separation – and it's been entirely successful. Come on, darling, we needed it. We both agreed. And Daddy's perfectly capable of looking after them, he really is, if that's what's really bothering you.

LOUISE: No, no, it isn't – well, it wouldn't if –

HARRY: If what?

LOUISE: Well, if only he'd listen! When I tried to explain about all the meals I'd left in the fridge, his eyes just glazed over, and I know he doesn't really believe dairy produce brings on Nigel's headaches, thinks diet's all a lot of faddish nonsense. Then when I got on to Ophelia and the boiled fish, I could see he wasn't taking in a word – he'll probably feed her scraps every time she miaows and then she won't want the fish and she'll go around the house crapping out those frightful worms again – *and* he'll ignore all the rules about television watching – they've both got school projects – Nigel's is bound to be awfully complicated, and Natalie would rather watch television than do anything . . .

HARRY: (*Interrupting soothingly*) Darling, darling, it'll be all right. We're back tomorrow . . .

LOUISE: I know, I know. Oh, I do wish I had a parent left of my own. Mummy would have adored having them.

HARRY: Well, Daddy adores it too.

LOUISE: (*With sudden dramatic tenderness*) You're beautiful!

HARRY: (*Looks at her*) Am I? Why did you say that, like that?

LOUISE: It was the curve of your mouth. It reminded me so much of Nigel's.

HARRY: My darling, you mustn't worry so much.

LOUISE: But I wasn't worrying! I was loving your mouth.

HARRY: I know. But you do – recently you've taken to it. Worrying. It makes my heart turn over.

LOUISE: (*Apprehensively*) What with?

HARRY: (*Laughs*) With worry, of course.

LOUISE: Well, *I* don't mind. People *should* worry about each other. Because worry is just love in its worst form. But it's still love.

HARRY: But you know, seriously, you know, darling –

LOUISE: (*Crying out*) What is it?

HARRY: Oh, nothing. But really, whether you shouldn't give your writing a bit of a rest. You've been at the same piece for over a year now – and you said in the car coming down that you keep going back and re-writing the same bit again and again –
(*There is a pause.*)

LOUISE: But I've just broken through at last. I know I have. I've even thought of a title – a wonderful title – *Roses are White*. (*Crying out in panic*) You can't want me to give it up! You can't!

HARRY: Darling, darling, darling! The last thing I want to do

is distress you, it was just a thought, an idle thought . . .
(*Moving towards her.*)

(DRAYCOTT *appears at the gate.*)

DRAYCOTT: Oh, here you are at last!

HARRY: (*Momentarily appalled*) Ted, what are you doing
here?

DRAYCOTT: Come to see you, of course. (*Entering*) Had a bit
of trouble as nobody in the bloody village seems to have
heard of any Pertwees, but then some old geezer outside
the pub said, 'Oh, you must mean the *weekenders*, them
that come up from London to lord it over Great
Yarcombe folk every few months or so with their
London ways and their – ' (*Makes drinking movements
with his elbow. Laughs. He is obviously in a state of
controlled tension.*)

HARRY: (*Attempts a little laugh*) Darling, this is Ted Draycott.

LOUISE: (*Attempting warmth*) How do you do, I'm a . . . a
great fan of yours.

HARRY: Have a splash of wine.

DRAYCOTT: Thanks.

HARRY: We are having lunch tomorrow, aren't we? The Gay
Hussar?

DRAYCOTT: That's right.

HARRY: Ah, I thought we were.

DRAYCOTT: But there were a number of things I suddenly
realized had to be chatted over *before* our lunch.

HARRY: I see.

LOUISE: Would you like me to . . . to go somewhere else?

HARRY: Absolutely not, I mean good God, darling –

DRAYCOTT: I certainly don't mind your hearing anything I've
got to say. It's not personal. It's business. I want to find
a new publisher, Harry.

HARRY: (*Shocked pause*) Ah. Well, you can probably guess
my feelings about that, Ted, but –

DRAYCOTT: (*Interrupting*) This isn't just the best thing I've
ever done, Harry, we both know it's that, but it's by far
the most commercial thing. Thirty thousand pounds

15

isn't good enough. Has he let you see it yet?

LOUISE: No, not yet – but I'm afraid I wouldn't know about advances, thirty thousand seems such a lot of money to me. (*Little laugh*) Actually far more than our house cost.

DRAYCOTT: Really? Well, once you've finished converting it from rural primitive to urban bijou its value will shoot up.

LOUISE: Urban bijou – we've restored it to exactly as it used to be – we haven't allowed –

HARRY: Yes, well I . . . I really don't think there's any point comparing the price of our house with Ted's novel –

DRAYCOTT: *Bugger All*. That's the title. (*To* LOUISE) I hate it when people refer to it as 'Ted's novel', it's not *my* novel any more, it's its own creature, which is *Bugger All*.

HARRY: Yes, sorry, anyway *Bugger All* is quite different from our house –

LOUISE: Little Paradise.

(HARRY *looks at her in surprise*.)

DRAYCOTT: What?

LOUISE: Our house is called Little Paradise.

HARRY: Ted, an advance is only an advance, it still has to be paid back out of royalties, and really thirty . . .

DRAYCOTT: It's not a question of the money, bloody hell, you know that better than anyone, Harry. People get to hear about the advance, it even gets into the newspapers. (*Draws breath. Defiantly*) I want sixty thousand for *Bugger All*.

HARRY: (*Stares at him in disbelief*) Well, that's quite a jump, Ted.

(RONNIE *appears at the gate. He is sweating profusely, controlling agitation*.)

LOUISE: (*Gratefully*) Ronnie – there you are!

RONNIE: (*Coming through gate*) I'm so sorry to be late – so sorry. Louise, my dear – Harry – so good to see you again – but am I interrupting? If so I can – my own fault for . . . for . . .

HARRY: You're not interrupting in the slightest.

(DRAYCOTT *laughs sardonically*.)

I mean, how can you be – as we've been waiting for you – um, oh, this is a friend from London, Ted Draycott, one of my best novelists.

RONNIE: Oh, how do you do? How do you do? (*Makes great social effort*.) Oh, good heavens, of course. I did so enjoy your last, I don't remember what it was called exactly, but I do remember the story very well, oh, very well – about this . . . this rather sensitive chap, wasn't it, who suddenly turns into an ape, I can't recall how it happened, but he keeps his human consciousness, that was the point, wasn't it, and goes on doing all these . . . these rather, um, things, but describes them in this rather sensitive fashion – all his sexual adventures and . . . and habits, um, most diverting and – or was it a monkey? (*He is mopping at himself with a handkerchief. There is a pause*.)

HARRY: (*With relief*) Oh, we need another glass.

LOUISE: I'll get it.

HARRY: No, no darling – (*Hurries in*.)

DRAYCOTT: It was a monkey. And it was called *Banana Love*.

RONNIE: *Banana Love*, yes, that's right. *Banana Love*.

DRAYCOTT: Sold twenty thousand in hardback, hundreds of thousands in paperback. Film rights. American rights. What you might call a bit of a success.

(HARRY, *meanwhile, in the house, has paused in the kitchen, and is standing in some ferment*.)

HARRY: Sixty thousand – sixty thousand! (*Gets a glass, then slumps into a chair*.)

RONNIE: Well, that sounds wonderful, wonderful!

DRAYCOTT: Wonderful for the author, certainly, her name is Lucinda Darkon.

RONNIE: Oh. I'm terribly sorry – of course that's quite right, a woman, I remember thinking how clever she must be, to take on the human male *and* the male ape – monkey – so . . . so what have you written? Would I have come across . . . ? I'm trying to build up a parish library, so any recommendation –

LOUISE: He's just finished a new one, Harry thinks it's quite remarkable, it's called *Bugger Off*!

RONNIE: *Bugger Off*, is it? Well, that's snappy enough.

DRAYCOTT: Actually it's called *Bugger All*!

RONNIE: Oh. Well, that's even snappier – anyway, just as snappy.

DRAYCOTT: Wouldn't quite fit into your parish library, though, would it?

RONNIE: Oh, I don't know – some of the folk around here are quite . . . quite fearless readers, old Mrs Durrant, for instance, she actually enjoyed the Old Testament, said it made her laugh aloud – and I'd make sure it didn't get into the wrong hands, of course.

DRAYCOTT: The wrong hands – oh, censor it, so to speak.

RONNIE: Well, no, not exactly censor, but only recommend it to . . . to people who care for that sort of thing.

DRAYCOTT: What sort of thing?

RONNIE: Well, like your novel. *Bugger All*.

DRAYCOTT: What is it like, my novel?

RONNIE: Well, I'm assuming – given its title – that it's pretty strong meat.

DRAYCOTT: And you wouldn't want strong meat to go down the wrong throats, eh?

RONNIE: Well, I wouldn't want anyone who might be upset by it to – well, to be upset by it.

DRAYCOTT: You don't believe in people being upset by literature then?

RONNIE: Not if they don't want to be. I mean, some people *like* being upset, and I'd press it on them, of course, and some people aren't really upset by anything, are they? So I'd press it on them.

DRAYCOTT: Thank you. Most kind. (*Goes and sits down, half-turned away from* RONNIE.)

LOUISE: (*Looks from one to the other*) Oh, I'd better go and find out just what's happened to Ronnie's glass. (*Hurries off.*)

RONNIE: I do hope I haven't given you offence.

DRAYCOTT: Yes, I expect you're against that too, eh?

RONNIE: Well, yes. As a matter of fact I am.

(DRAYCOTT *grunts sarcastically.*
RONNIE *makes to say something, but gives up.*
*Meanwhile in the house,* LOUISE *has stopped to draw breath, pull herself together, etc., then goes into kitchen.*)

LOUISE: What are you doing? Where's Ronnie's glass?

HARRY: What, darling? (*Recollecting himself.*) Oh. The glass, of course. I was just trying to sort out what's the best thing to do about Draycott – leaving Haylife and Forling is about his worst possible move . . .

LOUISE: But darling, we can't leave Ronnie out there alone with him. He's being so offensive – is he drunk, do you think? (*Getting the glass.*)

HARRY: No, I wish he were. He's quite sweet when he's drunk. But sixty . . . sixty . . . how can I possibly –

LOUISE: You *must* go back out, darling. It's not fair on Ronnie.

HARRY: Bugger Ronnie! Can't you see this is a crisis, for God's sake? I need a moment to think. To think. Is that too much to ask?

(LOUISE *looks at him, shocked and upset. She turns, goes through passage into sitting room, sits down on sofa.*
HARRY *makes a gesture of angry despair, thumping his fist down on arm of chair.*)

RONNIE: (*Abruptly, he is shaking*) I simply don't understand.

DRAYCOTT: What don't you understand?

RONNIE: How you can be so purposelessly rude. There's enough rudeness in the world, cruelty, people do such things to each other – often they think they've got a reason – they feel something . . . something . . . powerful – or drink – who knows, who knows where it comes from, the why of it, but you . . . you had no reason. You just see a chap – a vicar – and you think, why not have a bit of fun, sneer at him – to . . . to do what? Why? Does it make you feel better? Bigger? Stronger? A more important writer, and I'm just a vicar – no consequence – a joke, feeble, polite, eh? Is that it?

DRAYCOTT: Look, I drove all the way down here to have an extremely important conversation with my agent about changing publishers – and I end up having an absolutely asinine conversation with you about a book I didn't write, and then about how *you're* going to decide which of your bloody parishioners you'll allow to read my novels, that is, if you can remember their titles and who wrote them. How do you expect me to feel?

(HARRY *gets up, goes into sitting room.* LOUISE *looks up at him. They stare at each other for a moment.*)

RONNIE: Oh. Well, of course I didn't . . . didn't quite understand – how much you might feel – as far as I'm concerned anybody can read your books. Anybody who wants to, that is.

HARRY: Darling, I'm sorry, so sorry.

(LOUISE *gets up with a little cry. They embrace.*
DRAYCOTT *looks at* RONNIE *with contempt, turns away again.*)

RONNIE: I'm trying to apologize.

DRAYCOTT: But I don't want you to. I'd just like silence until I can conclude my conversation with Harry, and be on my way. All right?

(RONNIE *nods, makes to sit down, then suddenly hurls himself across at* DRAYCOTT, *seizes him by the lapels, shakes him about.*)

(*Incredulously, half-laughing*) What the – what the hell!

(*Struggles with* RONNIE, *overpowers him easily, getting him into a half-nelson as* RONNIE *continues to flail feebly.*)

HARRY: You were absolutely right. So let's get back and keep the party rolling, eh? (*Little laugh.*)

(*They go out of sitting room. As they do so,* LOUISE

20

*remembers the glass. She goes to collect it while* HARRY *steps outside.*)

(*Stands staring as* DRAYCOTT *and* RONNIE *struggle*) Good God! (*He hurries across garden.*) Get your hands off him – for God's sake, Ted – leave him! (*Pulls at* DRAYCOTT.) What the hell do you think you're doing?

(LOUISE *comes out on to the porch as* HARRY *succeeds in pulling* DRAYCOTT *free, and stands watching, shocked.*)

DRAYCOTT: Me doing? He . . . he . . . he attacked me!

(RONNIE *has partly collapsed, drags himself to chair.*)

HARRY: Are you all right?

RONNIE: (*Nods*) My . . . my fault – I . . . I . . .

(HARRY *turns, looks at* DRAYCOTT.)

LOUISE: (*Runs down*) How dare you! How dare you! You . . . you contemptible bully!

HARRY: Yes, I think you'd better clear off, Ted. You had no bloody business coming down here and muscling in on our Sunday anyway, and there'll be no need for you to do it again. You can find a new agent to find your new publisher for you, and I'll give you my last bit of professional advice. You haven't a hope in hell of getting sixty thousand for your book, Haylife and Forling wouldn't have come through with the thirty thousand in the end anyway, because frankly, Ted, the book's OK now that I've got you to cut and rewrite large parts of it, it'll get by, no more than that!

(*Pause.*)

DRAYCOTT: And I thought . . . I thought you were meant to be good with writers. (*Turns, walks off through the garden.*) And you (*To* RONNIE) you're just a little shit! A little shit in a dog collar! (*Slams gate.*)

(*There is a pause.*)

LOUISE: How are you feeling?

RONNIE: Better. Better, thank you.

HARRY: (*Pouring him wine*) Well, here you are. At last. (*Hands it to him.*) Better late than never, eh? (*Laughs shakily.*)

21

RONNIE: (*Takes glass, drains down wine*) Thank you. Thank
you so much, both of – both of – I'm terribly sorry – it
really was all . . . all my fault.

LOUISE: Nonsense, Ronnie. I heard the way he was talking
to you –

HARRY: And so did I! He was provoking you –

RONNIE: Yes, but he was an important client of yours, I
could tell, and he's quite right – in a way – a shit in a
dog collar. I mean, I mean, how can I speak of all the
things I'm meant to speak of, if I can't myself – the
Lord knows, my influence is feeble enough but if I can't
restrain myself from assaulting some chap simply
because he's being a bit . . . a bit oafish – and it wasn't
anything to do with him really. I was already in a state,
you see, because of . . . because of . . . (*Stops.*)

LOUISE: (*Exchanging glances with* HARRY) Oh, more upsets
from Wilemena?

RONNIE: No, no, not really, not Wilemena – well of course
she's always on my mind and she's been phoning a lot
recently with some rather strange – obscene, really – yes,
that's what they are, obscene messages. But . . . but no,
it wasn't her at all, it was because of this morning's
sermon, you see. On tolerance. Actually rather effective
for once, I thought. Anyway I made some strong points,
important around here where there is so much . . . so
much ignorance. And one or two of them even seemed
to be listening. And so after lunch I . . . I sat down in
my study and worked on it some more – I thought I
might turn it into a paper to give at the Honiton
Religious and Philosophical Society – we meet every . . .
every other week, you know – and . . . and I was really
quite involved, I felt that for once I was having a useful
Sunday, a useful Sunday and an enjoyable one, when the
door opened, and there was Mrs Mossop. I thought
she'd just come round to ask me if I'd enjoyed my pot
roast, she does that sometimes, you know, even though
Sunday is her day off, she cares so much. But it wasn't

that, not at all. She was in the most dreadful state. Dreadful. And all . . . all because she thought my sermon had been about *her*, can you believe! You see, the other day I'd reprimanded her, very gently, very gently, for something she happened to say about a Jewish family her nephew works for in Axminster. In their cheese shop. So she'd got it into her head that I was actually denouncing her from the pulpit! My dear Mrs Mossop, as if I could do such a thing! It took ages . . . ages to explain, to calm her down, I was nothing like as patient as I should have been, I kept thinking that I should have left to come over here, I'd been looking forward to it so much – such a long time since you were last down – and she still really wasn't quite . . . quite herself when I said I had to go, I really had to go. So I hurried over, knowing I hadn't really done right by her, and there he was, your novelist – and *he* didn't know any of that, of course – just being a bit oafish, that's all – so, yes. My fault. Yes. Yes. (*Nods*) A little shit in a dog collar. I'm deeply sorry. (*Little pause*) Sorry.

LOUISE: (*Puts her arm around him*) Oh, poor Ronnie. Nobody could be less like a little shit – and you've got absolutely nothing . . . nothing to be sorry about!

HARRY: In fact, you've done me a favour. We were bound to part company in the end, anyway. Better now than later. Here, Ronnie – (*Pours him another glass of wine.*)

RONNIE: Thank you . . . thank you – oh – what's the time – oh good God, I've got to be all the way to Lower Mudge, I'm taking Evensong and . . . and – I can't go looking like this, as if I've been in a brawl, which I have, got to get back and change – and I've been so looking forward – it's been months – how is everyone, old Ben? (*Getting up, putting glass down.*)

LOUISE: He's fine, fine, Ronnie.

HARRY: Yes, fine.

RONNIE: And Nigel and Natalie?

HARRY: They're fine too.

RONNIE: Well, please give them all my . . . my . . . (*Hurries towards gate*) my – (*Stops, turns at the gate*) So sorry. So sorry. (*Hurries out.*)

LOUISE: Poor Ronnie. (*Then sees* HARRY. *Pours him a glass of wine, brings it to him, as* HARRY *sits.*) Is it so very bad, my love? Losing him?

HARRY: Well, let's say it's come at a bad time. I – we could have done with our ten per cent of that thirty thousand. What with our mortgage here and in London. And it's a good novel, *Bugger All*. Dreadful title, but I could have got him to change that.

LOUISE: Well then, darling, shouldn't you try to patch it up?

HARRY: Absolutely not. You heard what I said to him about not getting even thirty thousand. He'll never forgive that. Especially as he knows it's true. Besides . . . besides, there comes a point, doesn't there, when you have to separate the important parts of your life. London is where I work. This is where we breathe together, you and I. (*Puts his arm around her.*) But it's taught us a valuable lesson. No more intruders down here, ever. (*Telephone rings.*)

That'll be Daddy.

LOUISE: (*Following* HARRY *to phone*) Oh, I hope nothing's the matter.

HARRY: Darling, he *said* he'd phone about now. (*Goes into sitting room, picks up phone.*) Hello? Yes, hello, Daddy, everything all right? Good. Yes, we are, thanks, very much – where are they, by the way? Oh, well don't let them watch too much, they know the rules, an hour an evening – what? Oh yes, that's right, two hours at weekends. Well, give them our love, Louise sends hers to you – what? Right, hang on, I'll tell her, she's right here. (*To* LOUISE) His compliments to the chef. The fish concoction you left them was especially scrumptious.

LOUISE: The fish? But that was for Ophelia. I told him – I told him – !

HARRY: Daddy, hello, now listen carefully. It's very important that you don't panic but there's a chance – just a chance – that you're going to need your stomachs pumped out, all of you. You see, that fish you ate was for the cat – Ophelia – and it had worm powder in it. Its effect on humans might be – what? Daddy, it's not funny! Listen to me! What? (*To* LOUISE) He says it was just a joke. Nigel's and Natalie's actually. (*On phone*) Well, thank God, Daddy, but tell the children – no, don't tell them anything – give them our love, see you tomorrow. (*Hangs up, goes to* LOUISE.) There, you see, I told you everything would be all right.

LOUISE: (*Emotionally*) Oh hold me, Harry, hold me, my love. (HARRY *comes across, puts his arms around her. She clasps at him.*)

HARRY: (*Overcome with love*) My darling – my dear, dear darling – everything *is* all right. You'll see.

### SCENE THREE

*Four years later. Mid-morning. In the drawing room, Louise's typewriter, with a typescript piled beside it. There are additional bits of furniture. In the kitchen various smart items have been added, including a small espresso machine. There are signs of breakfast debris on the table.*

*In the garden there are a few more pieces of light garden furniture, i.e. deck chairs, etc. The tree stump has been sawed level, and a round piece of wood attached to it, to make it into a table.*

NIGEL, *about sixteen, is on the swing, swinging gently as he reads. He begins, almost unconsciously, to swing higher and higher, standing up, still reading, as he does so. Still reading, he slows the swing down, drops neatly back on to his bum.*

NATALIE, *during this, has entered the sitting room from upstairs, slightly furtively. She is carrying a transistor and a large drawing pad, with which she is attempting to conceal the transistor. She looks around the room in relief, goes on through the corridor, enters kitchen with same furtiveness, and welcomes its emptiness. She takes an apple from the table, and comes carefully into the garden, checking it out as she does so.*

NATALIE: So, where is everyone?

NIGEL: Don't worry, you're safe. Daddy's driven into Honiton to get the provisions. Mummy's roaming the fields in search of inspiration. And Grandad's upstairs changing into his sabotage togs. We're going on another mission.

(NATALIE *has dropped into deck chair, taken out cigarettes, and lit one luxuriously while continuing to munch on an apple. She switches transistor on low.*)

NATALIE: You must be crazy.

NIGEL: Well actually he is. Completely crazy. But nobody seems to notice, except me.

(LOUISE *enters the sitting room, wearing a straw hat, in a state of agitation. She takes her hat off, tosses it on to sofa, looks at the typewriter, goes over to it, sits down and begins to assault it almost as if in desperation.*)

NATALIE: Christ, I've only just got up and I'm bored already. If only we could get a television set down here, at least.

NIGEL: (*Imitating* HARRY) 'Well, Nats, I think we could all do with a rest from the incessant bombardment of the senses' – (*Then imitating* LOUISE) 'I quite agree with Daddy, darling, we have ten and a half months of noise and trivia' – oh God, you know who gets back today, the Reverend Droopy-bum. I'll have to hear all about his travels through China – with long discussions about Communism and faith and – oh God, oh God.

NATALIE: Why do we call him the Reverend Droopy-bum?

NIGEL: Because it seemed funny when you thought it up ten years ago. Very childish. We really ought to show him more respect.

NATALIE: Yes, it's horrid, isn't it? What about – (*Thinks*) the Very Reverend Dribble-cock?

NIGEL: Much better.
> (*They sit gravely. Suddenly explode with laughter.*
> NATALIE *grinds out her cigarette carefully, and throws the butt into the bushes. She throws all succeeding butts into bushes.*)
> Poor old Ronnie! Anyway, I'm not going to do the churches with him any more. Can't face the thought.
> (*Suppresses slight shudder.*)

NATALIE: Thought you liked him really.

NIGEL: Oh, I do really. But he tries so hard to amuse and instruct, his eyes go sparkly and he even drools – anyway he seems to –

NATALIE: I expect he's drooling for you. After all, he's a vicar and you're such a pretty little chap. What are you going to do when he comes round 'just . . . just wondering if our young . . . young Nigel would . . . would care to have a peep at an odd – rather odd – charming little navel I stumbled across in . . . in St Turd's in . . . in Little Sodfuck over . . . over by – '

NIGEL: Don't know actually. Probably have to have one of my headaches coming on.
> (NATALIE *turns transistor up. It is pop music.*)
> Hey, be careful! She may be back.

NATALIE: (*Turns transistor down*) Oh God, oh God, listen – I *knew* they'd play it, knew it! (*Begins to move to the music, then gyrate in a parody of sexuality, cigarette hanging from her lips.*
> LOUISE, *during this, has lifted her head as if hearing something, gets up abruptly, stands for a second as if deciding what to do, goes towards kitchen.*
> *The doorbell goes, unheard by* NIGEL, *who has gone back to reading, and* NATALIE *who is dancing.* LOUISE *stops, surprised, goes back, and out, right.*
> *Natalie's dancing is becoming increasingly sexual.* NIGEL *glances at her furtively, then forces himself back to his book. During the following scene, he is unable to resist eyeing* NATALIE *covertly from time to time.*

LOUISE *re-enters the sitting room, followed by* NAOMI, *who is carrying an electric typewriter.*)

LOUISE: — To tell you the truth I'd forgotten Harry had someone coming down or I would have cleared my — here — (*Picking up her typescript*) have to be careful that they're in the right order — I never number the pages until I've finished a draft. Harry says that's very silly of me but really it's a superstition — there you are! Is that enough room? Oh, my typewriter — I'll put it . . . I'll put it — (*Moves it over to sofa*) there!

(NAOMI *puts her typewriter down in Louise's place. She is rather gauche, flustered.*)

You did say Leonie, didn't you?

NAOMI: No, Naomi. Naomi Hutchins.

LOUISE: Oh yes, aren't you the girl that went off to get married, Harry said was irreplaceable?

NAOMI: Well, no, that was Angela.

LOUISE: Oh, so you're Angela's replacement?

NAOMI: Well no, Angela's replacement is Debbie, she was going to come down today but her mother was taken ill — so I'm replacing her, really. I've never worked for Mr Pertwee before but . . . but she told me everything I had to do so I hope . . . I hope, um, is there a plug?

LOUISE: A plug?

NAOMI: I mean a . . . a socket. For the plug. For the typewriter. It's an electric —

LOUISE: Is it? Oh I see. Well, here's one, it's the nearest — here — (*Getting on her hands and knees.*) I'll take the lamp out — (*Takes lamp plug out, while* NAOMI *looks increasingly desperate*) now if you give me the plug — (*Holding up her hand. Waits, wagging her hand*) the plug.

NAOMI I haven't got one.

LOUISE: What?

NAOMI: I've . . . I've . . . I forgot it. It comes separately, you see, and I just . . . just picked up the typewriter without thinking.

LOUISE: (*Getting up*) Oh dear.

28

(*There is a pause.*)

NAOMI: What'll I do?

(LOUISE *fights a brief battle with herself.*)

LOUISE: Well, I suppose you'll have to manage with mine, won't you? It's rather old-fashioned, I'm afraid, but it's the only one I've ever had down here – actually it's rather personal – like a . . . like a fountain pen really. I've written great chunks of all my novels on it, you see.

NAOMI: (*Obviously relieved*) Oh, don't worry, I can work it all right, it'll do perfectly, thank you.

LOUISE: (*Gets it, puts it on the table*) Well then, there you are. Is there anything else? (*Controlling crossness.*)

NAOMI: No, I'm ready as soon as Mr Pertwee is.

LOUISE: Oh, well he's gone to Honiton – he'll be back any moment –

NAOMI: Well, there are one or two things Debbie gave me to type up. I'll get on with those. (*Opening briefcase.*)

LOUISE: Right. Well, I'll leave you then.

(LOUISE *goes to the door, left, turns and glances in pain as* NAOMI *sits down at her table, lifts lid off Louise's typewriter, opens briefcase, puts a sheet of paper in, takes out a document, and begins to type.*)

Is it all right?

NAOMI: (*Looks at* LOUISE) It's fine, thanks.

LOUISE: Good. (*Goes into kitchen, stands for a moment dealing with anger, frustration, etc., with the typewriter clacking away on right; music coming from garden, left.*

NATALIE *has now let herself go in sexy dance.* NIGEL *watches her, hypnotized, then suddenly turns the transistor off.*)

NATALIE: (*Turns, looks at him*) Bloody hell!

NIGEL: (*Almost as if bewildered himself*) Sorry. Sorry, Nat. It was . . . was . . . my head. Doing one of its things. Or something.

NATALIE: Probably because I'm so sexy. (*Putting transistor back on, low, begins to gyrate again.*)

29

NIGEL: (*Grins*) Yes, you are, aren't you? In your way.

NATALIE: Do you remember that time she caught us messing about in the bath and she said, 'Now, Nigel, little boys really shouldn't put their fingers up little girls – '

LOUISE: (*Goes on to porch, attempting calm manner, smiles with warm reproof*) Natalie darling, you're not actually smoking, are you? And with the transistor on. (*There is a pause.*)

NATALIE: (*Putting out cigarette*) Sorry, Mummy. (*Turns transistor off.*) It was so low we didn't think anybody could hear it.

LOUISE: It was right underneath my concentration, you see. Banging away. Like a headache. And anyway, we come here to get away from all that – pop and London and fashionable noises – we all had an agreement that we wouldn't – but *why* are you smoking? Apart from your health you know what'll happen to you at school if they catch you – Nigel, have you been?

NIGEL: Yes, Mummy. 'Fraid I have. We share them, you see.

LOUISE: Oh, it's so depressing, so depressing . . .
(NATALIE *has shot* NIGEL *a grateful glance.*)
– you know that Daddy and I would never dream of issuing prohibitions and orders, there's just been an agreement between us all, that's how we work as a family, through agreements. Daddy gave up smoking – not that he ever smoked much – but he couldn't bear the thought that he could be responsible –

NATALIE: Sorry, Mummy. You take them. So I won't be tempted.

LOUISE: (*Makes to take them, resists*) No, I can't do that. They're yours. Bought out of your pocket money. So I've no right to them, have I?

NATALIE: But I want you to take them, really I do. I don't want to smoke.

NIGEL: Yes, take them for *our* sake, Mummy. Please. (*Taking package from* NATALIE *and passing it to* LOUISE.)

LOUISE: All right. I will. If that's what you really want. But if you want them back –
NIGEL: We'll just ask – fair enough?
(NATALIE *grimaces*.)
LOUISE: Fair enough. (*Takes cigarettes, looks into package*.) There aren't any.
NIGEL: No, but it'll be a symbol, Mums. Keep it as a symbol.
NATALIE: (*Getting up*) I'll go and do a drawing now, shall I? Of that oak by the river. (*Picks up sketch pad, pencils, transistor*.)
LOUISE: A good idea, darling, it's the only way, practise, practise, practise – especially these days when the competition for art schools – but why are you taking that with you? You're not going to play it out on the river –
NATALIE: No, no, of course not, Mums – I'll leave it here. (*Throws transistor on to the lawn, runs angrily off towards the gate*.)
(*There is a pause, as* LOUISE *stares after* NATALIE.)
LOUISE: Why did she do that? We gave it to her – it was our birthday present – we're not against her playing anything she wants to listen to, even pop. It's only down here we objected to. And she agreed. Because of other people –
NIGEL: (*Switches it off*) There you are, plays perfectly. You know, Mums, you really shouldn't worry about everything so much.
LOUISE: I know, I know. I wish I didn't, too. (*Sits down in deck chair, smiles at* NIGEL.) But I bet . . . I bet anything you like –
NIGEL: What, Mums?
LOUISE: That you didn't smoke a single half of a fraction of a cigarette, did you?
NIGEL: (*After a little pause*) But if people just let people do and be what they want –
LOUISE: But if you love them –

NIGEL: Well, that's why you have to let them, I suppose. I mean, if you don't everybody just gets more upset and then things get worse, don't they?

LOUISE: You sound just like your father. (*Turns away, upset.*)

(*During this,* NAOMI *has been typing steadily but uneasily, pausing at one point to light a cigarette, which she puffs at furiously, then can't find an ashtray to extinguish it. Becomes panicky when she hears footsteps off, right. Grinds butt out on the sole of her shoes, jams the butt into briefcase, waves her hand about, and resumes typing.*

BEN *enters. He is wearing tweeds, and is carrying wellington boots in his hand. Sees* NAOMI *at typewriter.*)

BEN: Top of the morning, Lou, old girl! Trout tonight, I promise you! And if not trout, frogs' legs! (*Laughs loudly, goes on into passage,* NAOMI *staring after him.*)

NIGEL: I'm sorry, Mums. (*Goes to her, puts his arms around her.*) We're all jolly pleased you worry so much about us – well, love us so much, anyway.

LOUISE: (*Voice trembling*) But you're right. I know you're right, you and Daddy. I don't know why I get so . . . so . . . feel so – all the time – just at the moment. (*Stares at* NIGEL *pleadingly.*)

(BEN *bursts on to porch, carrying two fishing rods and with his boots on, singing.*)

BEN: Hey-ho, hey-ho, it's off to fish we go, with a la-la-la and a la-la-la, la-la, la – (*Stops, stares at* LOUISE *in amazement.*) Good God, what are you doing out here, old girl?

LOUISE: What do you mean?

BEN: Well, I saw you at it – in there – just a minute ago –

LOUISE: What do you mean at it?

BEN: Well, at your typewriter. Firing away on all cylinders. (*Clearly genuinely shaken.*)

LOUISE: No, no, it's just a girl for Harry – from the office –

BEN: Oh, well that explains it! (*Relieved.*) Thought for a moment might be a ghost – though I suppose as you're alive you couldn't really have a ghost yet, could you?

NIGEL: (*Indicating* LOUISE) How do you know this one isn't the ghost –

LOUISE: (*Laughs*) Oh, stop it, Nigel – I may not feel perfectly real today, but I'm here – it's such a pity we have to have office people down though –

BEN: Especially on a day like this! Have you ever known such a summer, eh? On and on, day after day –

LOUISE: (*Interrupting*) Well, to tell you the truth, Ben, it's beginning to get on my nerves, a bit. It's . . . it's so unEnglish. And all the poor farmers are in despair.

BEN: Oh, don't worry about them, they're always in despair, old girl. Hey, look at this, Nig, how did that get tangled up? (*Settles into a deck chair, begins to sort out one of the lines.*) Here, take this end – what a mess – (*Hands bit of line to* NIGEL.) Here, you hang on to this bit, old girl – (*Hands another bit to* LOUISE) that's how they get their subsidies to spend on those damn machines for destroying our countryside. Yes, vandals on tractors – and they dare to moan about the rest of us having a lovely summer – I tell you what I'd like to do to them – (NIGEL *gives him a warning glance to stop him.*

*During this* NAOMI *has stopped typing. She has sat with her head in her hands, then taken out another cigarette, lit it, inhaled briskly a few times, stubbed it out as before, and put stub into briefcase. As she does so, sees mirror in briefcase, takes it out, inspects her face, takes out comb, combs her hair, then stares into the mirror, and is depressed by what she sees.*)

(*Taking in Nigel's look, changes tack*) Don't understand, Nig, when we put them away they're all neat and ready to go for the next morning – (*Fumbles in pocket for knife, and takes it out*) but when we start off they're in a muddle. (*Laughs.*) Ooops, no, here's the problem – (*Opening knife, slashing it down clumsily.*)

(NIGEL *jumps, lets out a yelp.*)

LOUISE: Oh God, Ben, what have you done?

(BEN *stands, looking bewildered.*)

NIGEL: Oh, it's all right – (*Sucks at hand.*) Just a little cut.

LOUISE: Here, let me see.

BEN: I'm terribly sorry, Nig – I don't know how I . . . I . . .

NIGEL: You see, it's nothing, Mummy. Honestly.

LOUISE: It needs a plaster. And some antiseptic.

(*She goes into the house to the kitchen and opens cupboard door, as* NAOMI, *hearing her, resumes typing.*)

BEN: (*Quickly*) Old Tomalin's got his tractor in his field, just up the road. Been waiting for it all summer. Today's the day we'll get him. The old bully, we'll teach him to turn his cattle on you and Nat!

NIGEL: But that was years ago, Grandad. And anyway he didn't. We weren't anywhere near his cattle, we were hiding in the bushes here all the time, remember?

BEN: What? Well, he didn't care whether you were in our bushes or in his field, *that's* what I remember, Nig.

(*Sits in swing, begins to swing.*

NIGEL *glances at him worriedly as he continues to untangle line.*

LOUISE, *having got antiseptic, bandage, etc., stares towards sitting-room door. Then, as if unable to resist, she goes through the passage and opens the sitting-room door.* NAOMI *goes on typing as if unaware.* LOUISE *glares at her, makes to speak, doesn't, goes out.* NAOMI *stares after her, then goes back to typing.*)

(*Suddenly*) God, you know what I'd really love to do, get every farmer in the neighbourhood into the church hall and then blow them across the landscape, so you'd find a head or a foot in every ditch, that'd start the birds singing again! (*Begins to swing more violently.*)

NIGEL: (*Carefully*) You know, Grandad, I don't expect they mean any harm, they probably don't realize what they're doing. I mean, we shouldn't really *hate* them, should we?

BEN: What's the matter with you, Nig? Not losing your nerve, are you?

(NIGEL *makes to speak.* LOUISE *comes out into the garden.*)

34

LOUISE: Now, let's see it, darling –

NIGEL: (*Puzzled*) What?

> (*During the following* NAOMI *abandons typing, defiantly pulls out another cigarette, lights it, then sits smoking, hunched in tension and misery, dropping ash on floor and scuffing it with her foot.*)

LOUISE: Your hand, darling.

NIGEL: Oh. (*Holds it out.*)

> (LOUISE *peers at it, then begins to apply antiseptic.*)

No, it's here, Mummy. That's an old one.

LOUISE: Oh, yes. I see. (*Applies antiseptic, puts on elastoplast.*) There. You know you can't be too careful, you can get tetanus from the slightest scratch, just a bit of earth in the wound –

NIGEL: No, I know. Thank you, Mummy. Ready, Grandad?

BEN: (*Leaps off the swing*) Sir! (*Salutes.*)

LOUISE: But you'll be back in time for lunch, won't you?

BEN: It's already half-eleven, Lou. Don't worry, we'll repair to the Yeoman for cottage pie, and a tankard of – of good brown Coca-Cola, eh, Nig? All ready?

NIGEL: All ready, Grandad.

BEN: (*Meaningfully*) Have we got everything?

NIGEL: (*Realizing*) Well, perhaps I'd better get us a hat.

LOUISE: Yes, you must keep your head covered, darling. You know what the heat does to you.

> (NIGEL *goes into the kitchen. He searches for sugar, finds it, wraps up two packages of lumps, and puts them into his pocket. Goes into passage between hall and kitchen.*)

BEN: Coming along all right, the novel?

LOUISE: (*Making an effort*) Oh, well it's beginning to take on its own life. That's the main thing. The trouble is that when it does that, I can't control it unless I'm allowed to keep my grip on it whenever I want to – (*Suddenly spots one of Natalie's cigarette ends.*) Oh, I do wish she wouldn't do that! (*Picking it up, looking for others.*)

BEN: Sounds a bit like riding a horse.

LOUISE: It's not at all like riding a horse, Ben. At least in my experience. Not that I've ever ridden a horse. (*Looking for other cigarette butts.*)

BEN: Well, you have the sense of all this power under you – and if he's a firey brute –

LOUISE: (*Finding another one, and continuing to look*) Do you mind, Ben, would you mind very much (*Tightly*) if we didn't talk about my novel. Especially when I'm so desperate to get back to it! (*Finds another one.*) I don't know how she could! As if the whole place were . . . were her personal ashtray! (*Continues to look for butts, as* BEN *sits on swing, and begins to swing more and more steeply.*

NAOMI *meanwhile has heard* NIGEL *rooting about in passage, and makes to stub out the cigarette, but is too late.*)

NIGEL: (*Enters, carrying a hat*) Oh, hello.

NAOMI: Hello. (*Relieved.*)

NIGEL: Do you mind if I just look for another hat –

NAOMI: Of course.

NIGEL: I think my sister had it last – oh no, there it is, must have been Mummy – (*Takes hat up off sofa.*) There we are. I'm Nigel, by the way, Nigel Pertwee.

NAOMI: I'm your Dad's secretary. Temporary, that is. Naomi Hutchins.

NIGEL: Is there anything I can get you, Miss Hutchins?

NAOMI: No, thanks – oh well, if there's an ashtray?

NIGEL: Um, well, (*Goes to toby jug on mantelpiece*) what my sister does is she spits into this and then just drops them in – if you follow.

NAOMI: (*Gratefully*) Thanks.

NIGEL: Well, um. (*Goes out.*)

(NAOMI *spits into mug, drops butt in, and lights another one.*)

LOUISE: (*Who has been irritably conscious of Ben's swinging, is suddenly unable to stop herself*) Oh, do be careful on that swing, Ben. You're much heavier than the children and I'm sure it's weakening the rope.

(NIGEL *comes into garden, carrying hats.*)

36

NIGEL: There you are, Grandad. (*Handing him hat.*)

LOUISE: What, no, no, I meant for you, darling –

NIGEL: I've got one, Mummy. (*Putting other hat on his head, grabbing fishing rods, hands one to* BEN.) Come on then, Grandad, Hey-ho, hey-ho, it's off to fish we go, with a ta-la-la, and a tra-la-la, hey-ho, hey-ho, hey-ho –
(NIGEL *and* BEN *march down the garden, singing.* LOUISE *stares after them, and calls out.*)

LOUISE: Please be back in time for tea – or I shall worry!
(*After a little pause, as their voices recede, looks down at butts in her hand, makes to go to kitchen, looks towards sitting room, and throws the butts into the bushes with an angry and despairing gesture.*
*During this,* NAOMI *has pulled herself together, and with an air of determination, started typing.*
LOUISE *stands, listening to noise of typewriter, then goes to swing, and sits on it.*
HARRY *enters, his arms full of shopping. He stands there, staring at* NAOMI, *who after a few seconds, stops typing, and looks towards him apprehensively.*)

HARRY: (*In a frantic whisper*) What the hell are you doing here?

NAOMI: It's all right, I'm replacing Debbie. Her mother's been taken ill suddenly and she's gone to spend the weekend –

HARRY: Debbie's mother lives in Australia. (*Puts down shopping.*)

NAOMI: No, I mean that's what I told your wife. You're angry with me then. (*Stares at him.*) I'm sorry, Harry. I *had* to see you. I thought I'd go mad if I didn't. (*Stares at him pleadingly.*)

HARRY: Where's everybody else?

NAOMI: Don't know. They keep going through there. (*Points to door left.*)

HARRY: Who?

NAOMI: Well, your son and . . . and . . . your wife. And her father, I suppose it was.

37

HARRY: *My* father. So they're all here then!

NAOMI: Do you want me to leave?

HARRY: Yes, yes, you must – no, you mustn't, of course you mustn't, how could I explain – we'll just have to . . . have to . . .

NAOMI: I'm sorry, I couldn't help it, when Debbie said she was coming down it seemed like . . . like a gift, you see, a chance to . . . to . . . (*Looks at him yearningly.*)

HARRY: (*Suddenly realizing*) What on earth did you tell Debbie?

(NAOMI *looks at him miserably.*)

Oh, you didn't. Not about us. You couldn't have – for God's sake, she'll tell everybody, everybody, the whole office will be abuzz with my . . . my . . .

NAOMI: She understands, Debbie understands, I made her swear, swear, cross her heart, honestly, I promise!

HARRY: Sssh! Ssssh!

(*There is a pause.*)

NAOMI: (*Bursts out in a whisper*) I don't understand it, any of it, you couldn't keep your hands off me, you even said things, wonderful things, you said you'd never known anything like it, you said it was as if you'd been smitten, smitten by the hand of God, you said every time you looked at me, thought about me even, it made you go all hard –

HARRY: I know, I know, yes, I know, I'm sorry, Debbie – Naomi. Sorry. The thing is it was all true – it really was – as if I'd been smitten by something outside my . . . my . . . but you've seen for yourself why I can't any longer, why I had to stop – my wife, my son, my father, and I have a daughter, Natalie –

NAOMI: And me! You've got me too! Because I'm not going to let you go. I've never loved anyone before in my life. It wasn't just you that was smitten, it happened to me too, but for me it wasn't God. It was you! You can't just do all that to me and then shove me aside, something shameful that never really happened. It did happen! I'm

38

in your life and . . . and I'm not going to leave it! (*Stares at him, then starts to cry.*)

HARRY: Oh Christ, don't cry, don't cry, please don't cry!
(NAOMI *fumbles in briefcase, takes Kleenex out, wipes eyes, and blows nose.*)
Look, I'll just . . . I'll just – hang on a minute, I'll be right back!
(HARRY *hurries with furtive speed through passage, enters the kitchen carefully but nonchalantly – just in case – and then sidles on to the porch, and looks at* LOUISE *swinging. Withdraws quickly, hurries back through kitchen and passage to* NAOMI.
NAOMI *is still bringing herself under control, stuffing used Kleenex back into briefcase, taking out fresh ones.*)
Yes, they're out there, all of them, the vicar too, they're bound to come in a minute, any minute, we can't, we really can't talk now, not like this, listen my . . . my
. . . when I get back to London we'll talk properly, I promise, we'll have dinner even. All right? We'll really
. . . really – but now . . . now what we've got to do is –
now you go up to the bathroom, top of the stairs, first door on the left, and get yourself, um (*Gesturing to his face*) and I'll just go outside and say hello to everybody and then we'll do some work together, exactly as . . . as
. . . Debbie did give you all the contracts and other stuff, didn't she?
(NAOMI, *snivelling, nods.*
*During this,* LOUISE *jumps off the swing, and walks angrily and purposefully towards the porch.*)

NAOMI: I don't want to hurt you, you know. I don't want to hurt you.

HARRY: Of course you don't, of course you don't. I know that. But we'll sort everything out in London, don't you worry. Off you go then. (*Gives her a gentle shove.*) First door on the left upstairs, OK?
(NAOMI *leaves.*
LOUISE *has come on to the porch, hesitates, then girds*

*herself, and is about to go into the kitchen.*)

RONNIE: (*Appears at the gate*) Hello, Lou.

(HARRY *stands for a moment, pulls himself together, picks up shopping, makes as if to go to kitchen, thinks, and goes instead out through door right.*

LOUISE *turns around, stares at* RONNIE, *as if not recognizing him.*)

Sorry, did I . . . did I alarm you?

LOUISE: No, no, I was – expecting Harry, you see. Back with the shopping. (*Goes to him, and kisses him.*) How lovely to see you, Ronnie. (*Still rather absent.*) Um, well, how are you?

RONNIE: Very well. Very well indeed.

LOUISE: Oh good. Good. Yes, you look (*Gestures*) splendid.

RONNIE: And how are you?

LOUISE: Oh, fine, thanks. Well, actually (*Laughs*) I'd just worked myself up into having a scene with Harry's little secretary. She's rather taken over the sitting room, filling it with cigarette smoke, and my . . . my . . . actually dreadfully trivial of me – I can't bear the thought of her using my typewriter and having to sit here listening to it was driving me – (*Gestures*) so your turning up at the right moment has probably saved me weeks of embarrassment.

RONNIE: Well, that's the first time I've been able to see myself as . . . as in any way providential. Actually I've only popped over briefly, to welcome myself back, so to speak, and to let old Nigel know I hadn't forgotten our date – I promised him the first thing I'd do when I got back was to show him that little church in Lower Midgely – with such a charming font – and there's an organ, you know, dates back to 1803 – and the graveyard, they say Thomas Hardy once actually wrote a poem –

LOUISE: Oh well, he's gone off fishing with Ben.

RONNIE: Really, fishing? Well, I wouldn't have thought there was any water left for fish.

40

HARRY: (*Appears at the gate with the shopping*) Oh hello,
Ronnie!

RONNIE: Harry. Here, let me – (*Holds the gate open*) can I –
(*Offers to take bags.*)

HARRY: No, I'm all right, thanks. I'll just dump them in the
kitchen – oh, has Naomi turned up yet, darling?

LOUISE: Yes, she's in the sitting room. Having to make do
with my typewriter, darling, as she's brought down the
wrong one – but then it's not her fault, as she's not
Naomi, um, Debbie, I think her name is, anyway she's
not the one you're expecting.

HARRY: Right, well in that case I probably won't keep her
long – see you soon, Ronnie, longing to hear all about
Japan. (*Goes up, puts bags in the kitchen.*)

LOUISE: Japan – oh, Ronnie, I'm so sorry. I'd completely
forgotten – and Japan of all places.

RONNIE: Um, actually it was China. Though as a
matter of fact I didn't quite make it all the way to
China, either.

LOUISE: Oh. Well, where did you go?

RONNIE: Well, Southsea, as a matter of fact.

(*HARRY has gone into the sitting room. Finds it empty.
He strides about impatiently, then sees Naomi's
cigarettes on desk. He hesitates, then rather furtively
takes one, lights it, sits down and begins to go through
some papers.*)

You see, I rather stupidly told Wilemena my plans, I
was so excited that I just blabbed them out without
thinking of the consequences, and so she suddenly
insisted that she would come too – I got the hospital to
veto that of course, but they did say she was up to a
little holiday on the coast so I had to . . . had to scrap
China. And book Southsea instead.

LOUISE: Oh, what a pity. But at least this wonderful
weather –

RONNIE: Yes. Oh yes. Lovely. It was all quite, um, (*Lets out
a sudden whinny of laughter*) sorry, Louise! (*Then laughs*

*again.*) It was a nightmare, actually, an absolute nightmare! You see, it turned out that what poor Willie had in mind was a second honeymoon. And so first we spent a day in London buying a rather . . . rather . . . (*Gestures.*) She knew about these special shops – she'd cut out advertisements from some . . . some magazines, I must find out how she got hold of them as they have such an inflammatory effect on her imagination – and you can imagine some of the . . . the – hideously embarrassing. I was terrified I'd be glimpsed by one of my parishioners coming out of one of those shops accompanied by a rather eccentric trollope – well, that's what she looked like, as she'd had her hair hennaed. It was such a relief to get her to Southsea, into the hotel – behind locked doors, so to speak. Though on the other hand the intimacy – she spent most of the first day parading around in those garments, and trying to make the implements work. Fortunately she didn't realize that they required batteries – and I didn't tell her – but in the end I managed to get hold of one of her doctors, one of the more sensible ones, who sent some pills down on the train, so from then on it was really comparatively calm – except once or twice, but the manageress was really remarkably understanding. It turned out her own daughter had been a manic-depressive, thank God.

LOUISE: Oh Ronnie, how dreadful for you. I'm so sorry. So sorry.

RONNIE: Anyway, anyway, here I am, back to sanity again, back with my dear old Mrs Mossop again – and back in this garden again. (*Looks around garden, drinking it in.*)

LOUISE: (*Absently, almost automatically*) Yes, yes, you've kept it up beautifully, Ronnie. We've hardly had to touch it while you've been away.

RONNIE: Heavens, I love it, Lou! I've always loved it, but just before I left something . . . something rather special happened in it – the memory of it kept me going during the worst times in . . . in . . . Southsea. It was evening, you see, and I was – well, in that corner, over there, where the hollyhocks are, doing a spot of weeding. (*Points*.) I stood up, rather too quickly, I suppose, momentarily a touch dizzy – a touch *something* – or touched *by* something – and the house, the garden – well, you remember that first afternoon when we all met, and Nigel and Natalie were here hiding all the time, but you were so frightened and thought they'd been trampled to death by old Tomalin's cattle – and when we came back, all of us absolutely distraught, convinced they were dead – we suddenly heard them, their voices, they were laughing, and so was Ben – and you and Harry. I don't think I've ever seen such joy on human faces. Well, that evening I heard it all again. Seemed to hear it all again, their laughter, and the sun suddenly – in the twilight – it was suddenly so strong, and I felt your joy again, and I thought, yes, I thought, there is a spirit. A human spirit, a divine spirit even, they meet sometimes, by accident, if you're lucky. Or a touch dizzy. In an English garden. I know, oh, I know it's not much – only a second – but it happened. It could happen again. It's happened once or twice before. Particularly when I was a boy. Actually that's why I took Holy Orders. Perhaps I shouldn't have done. As I spend the rest of my time, all the time when nothing happens, being just a kind of social worker in funny clothes. But I thought a lot about that, Lou, in Southsea – and I realized that the funny clothes help me. Especially when . . . when one of my parishioners wants advice. And they do sometimes, Lou, they do come to me now and then – and it gives them permission, my dog collar gives them permission to take my advice when I'm telling them to be selfish. To live for themselves. Why, if it hadn't been for my dog collar, Mrs Mardock would never have agreed to leave her husband and he'd still be beating her, and the children would probably be in care. So you see, Lou –

LOUISE: Thought they were dead? I'd forgotten – yes, yes, that's right, Ben had put them in a field with some bulls, hadn't he? It was terrible, terrible – and yet we were happy then, we must have been – the joy on our faces – you said so. The children laughing. Joy and laughter! So we must have been happy! All of us. Even though everything was so uncertain – the future, I mean. So why . . . why is it all going wrong?

RONNIE: Going wrong? What's going wrong, Lou?

LOUISE: I don't know, I don't know. But something. Something's crept into our lives and . . . and they keep telling me not to worry so much, it's bad for me and bad for them and bad for everybody. But it isn't worry, Ronnie, it's worse than that. It's dread. That's what it is, dread. And I can't tell anyone, nobody seems to understand, nobody seems to care – oh, Ronnie, I'm so frightened! (*Bursts into sudden uncontrolled weeping.* RONNIE *hesitates, goes over, puts him arms around her.* NAOMI *enters. She has an air of sudden authority.*)

NAOMI: I've decided. We can't go on. For my sake, not for yours.

(HARRY *puts down papers, and stares at her transfixed. Gets up, goes over, takes her in his arms.* NAOMI *struggles briefly, then almost in spite of herself, responds. They kiss each other greedily.*

NATALIE *appears at the gate, opens it, stares for a second at* RONNIE *holding* LOUISE, *hesitates, then turns, hurries away.*

HARRY *and* NAOMI *separate, look at each other again.*) Smitten. Smitten by God.

HARRY: By the hand of God. (*Seizes her again.*) We must be careful. Just one more . . . one more kiss – (*They kiss.* NATALIE *opens door, a cigarette between her lips, stands staring at* HARRY *and* NAOMI, *then hurriedly closes door.*)

RONNIE: My poor, poor Louise, I'm sure everything's all right really – you must trust . . . trust . . .

LOUISE: (*Half laughing in tears*) What, Ronnie? In God?

RONNIE: Well, at least in your friends. In those who love you. In . . . in that part of life.

BEN: (*Off*) Hello – hello, anybody – help . . . help . . .

(RONNIE *and* LOUISE *turn as* BEN *and* NIGEL *appear at gate.* BEN *is supporting* NIGEL, *who is semi-conscious, bleeding from the head, his trousers torn, bleeding from his leg.*)

Help me – help me – there we are, old Harry, there, there, old son – you're home now. Everything'll be right as rain, right as rain –

(RONNIE *and* LOUISE *have run to the gate, opened it, and help* NIGEL *in, as* BEN *staggers after them, trembling and exhausted.*)

LOUISE: Oh, my God, oh my darling – (*Cradling Nigel's head. He has slumped to the grass.*) What happened, what happened?

BEN: It was the bull – one of Tomalin's bloody bulls – just thundered up out of nowhere and threw him . . . threw him . . .

NIGEL: I'm all right, Mummy. All right. Honestly.

LOUISE: Oh, my darling – my poor darling – get Harry! (*To* RONNIE.) Get Harry!

(RONNIE *runs up the garden.*)

BEN: There was this damned thresher, you see – for cutting down our hedgerows – alone in the field. We were just dropping a few sugar cubes in the tank to immobilize – didn't mean any harm – old Tomalin must have seen us, turned the bull on us, that's what he must have done! Enemy, you see. Fortunes of war. Of war. (*Gives* LOUISE *a ghastly grin.*) He'll be all right, Lou!

LOUISE: Oh, you fool, oh, you bloody fool, oh you bloody old fool. I always knew you'd be the death of someone – I always knew – Harry, hurry, Harry, Harry – (*Screaming.*

NATALIE *appears at gate, stares in shock.*
HARRY *and* NAOMI *have started kissing again.*)
Harry! (*Dreadful scream.* HARRY *stops mid-kiss, still holding* NAOMI, *looks around vaguely.* RONNIE *enters.*)

# ACT TWO

## SCENE ONE

*Two years later. Mid-morning. Sitting room and kitchen empty, though work is clearly in progress at the table, with a sheet in the typewriter, and pages on the table. A television set has been added to the room.*

NATALIE *enters sitting room, furtively. Hurries to the telephone, dials, speaks in a low voice, her words inaudible. She hangs up, makes a face of despair, goes through the kitchen, and out into the garden. She slumps on the swing, then begins to swing, with increasing violence, and as she does so chanting, 'Bugger, bugger', but not loudly, to herself.*

LOUISE *comes through the door, right, carrying a carrier bag. She stops at the table, glances down at the page in the typewriter, types a couple of words, then hurries through into the kitchen. She takes out a couple of chickens from the carrier bag, looks at them in disgust, turns on the oven, puts the chickens into a baking dish, smears butter over them, sprinkles salt, shoves them into the oven, all this at slapdash speed. She turns towards the door, to go to the sitting room, suddenly remembers, and turns back to the oven.*

BEN, *meanwhile, enters the sitting room, glances around anxiously, then goes on towards the kitchen. He opens the door just as* LOUISE *turns back to the oven. He closes the door quickly, goes back to the sitting room as* LOUISE *takes chickens out, scoops inside them, brings out the giblets in plastic bags, shudders, tosses them into the fridge, shoves the chickens back into the oven, rinses her hands, and goes into the sitting room, just as* BEN *is about to retreat upstairs.* BEN *turns around as the door opens, and pretends to be advancing.*

BEN: Morning, Louise, morning! Seem to be up a bit on the late side, country air, eh? Unused to it.

LOUISE: (*Unenthusiastically*) You must be desperate for a cup of coffee, I'll make you one.

BEN: No, no, don't trouble yourself. I can do it myself, perfectly capable.

47

LOUISE: Well, you'd probably rather have the kitchen to yourself, the paper's in there somewhere – oh, I've put the chickens in, so we can have lunch as soon as they get here – if you're thinking of eating anything.

BEN: Righto. Pretty well given up breakfasts anyway. Old stomach (*Slapping it*) getting a bit old, eh? (*Chuckles meaninglessly, goes into kitchen.*)

(LOUISE, *letting out audible sigh of relief, settles eagerly at the table.*

BEN *in the kitchen, fills the kettle, gets down a mug, plops a teabag into it, then sinks into a chair in despair, not putting the kettle on.*

RONNIE, *meanwhile, has come into the garden, sits down, almost as if not noticing* NATALIE. *He is clearly depressed.*

NATALIE *sees him, continues chanting, then swings down and leaps in front of him.*)

NATALIE: Aren't you at least impressed? Or shocked even? A well-brought-up young lady chanting obscenities at the vicar!

RONNIE: What? Sorry – oh (*Attempts a laugh*) actually it looked really quite . . . quite gymnastic.

NATALIE: It's what they call therapy, innit? You know, get rid of all the bad feelings and stuff.

RONNIE: And did you?

NATALIE: No. I've just had some disgusting news. Can I practise breaking it on you?

RONNIE: If you think I should be the first to know. (*Sits down on stump, which has now been converted into garden seat.*)

NATALIE: Well, at least you won't give me a miserable time – I'm pregnant, Ronnie.

RONNIE: (*Stares at her*) Well, well, um –

NATALIE: So what are your views on abortion?

RONNIE: Um, well there are . . . there are two views really. The official Church of England view and – well, mine. They're slightly contradictory but I try to hold them both. You see, Natalie, I do believe . . . do believe –

that on the one hand all life is sacred. And that on the other – well, we have to think – however painfully – what's best . . . best . . .

NATALIE: It's all right, Ronnie. You don't have to believe anything. I'm not pregnant really. It's far, far worse than that. I've failed all my A levels. Every fucking one of them.

RONNIE: (*Laughs in relief*) Oh.

NATALIE: I mean the whole fucking lot. And that's not funny, Ronnie.

RONNIE: No, of course it isn't – I was just – all of them. Oh dear, did you really? All of them?

NATALIE: (*Lighting a cigarette*) Except for scraping a C in Drama and a C in biology and a C in English. And that's fail in this family, fail is not getting As in everything you don't get scholarships in and then not going on to Cambridge to win prizes. Not doing that is failure in this family.

RONNIE: But you don't really want to go to Cambridge, do you?

NATALIE: Good Christ, no! In fact, I don't really need A levels for what I want to do.

RONNIE: And what's that?

NATALIE: Screw around, have a good time, shoot up in loos all over London, then get myself knocked up, live in a council house off state hand-outs, with three kids by different dads, that sort of thing.

RONNIE: Well then, you'd better start working on it, hadn't you? You won't achieve all that sitting in a swing in a garden in Devon.

(NATALIE *laughs*.)

Is everyone down this time?

NATALIE: No, just Mummy and me last night on the train. Daddy and Nigel are driving down now probably. Daddy had to stay on in London, you see. Last night. Haven't you noticed that's the way we usually do it now? So Daddy gets that extra night in London. And

49

Nigel gets that extra night in Cambridge. And they both get that extra night not being down here with Mummy and me. In Little Paradise.

RONNIE: Oh, but once they're here they always . . . always – and how's your grandfather, still not too keen on . . . on resuming country life?

NATALIE: No, he's here. Came down with Mummy and me.

RONNIE: Really? I am pleased! I've missed him – so he's over it all at last then, is he? That's good.

NATALIE: Well, it took a bit of time. He wouldn't answer the phone and whenever Daddy went round he either wasn't in or pretended he wasn't. It went on for months and months and months. And then suddenly he rang up and – anyway, he'll tell you himself, he's particularly keen to see you – in fact, you're the main reason he wanted to come.

RONNIE: Oh. Well, I'll look forward to – your mother's working, I suppose.

NATALIE: Don't know. She went down to the post office to pick up the chickens. (*Lifts a finger.*) Listen.
(LOUISE, *who has paused, starts typing again.*)
No, she's back. The typewriter. Can't you hear it?

RONNIE: No.

NATALIE: Sometimes I'm not sure whether I can actually *hear* it either. It's just something that I know is happening. Perhaps because it usually is. Like a mild headache. Do you want me to tell her you're here, or would you rather go in and let her see you?

RONNIE: Well, I don't want to disturb –

NATALIE: Good. Then you can answer my question, Ronnie.

RONNIE: About abortion? I thought I already had.

NATALIE: No, no. About me. Do you think there's a chance I'm adopted?

RONNIE: (*After a little pause*) I can't hold out much hope, I'm afraid.

NATALIE: (*Laughs*) Nigel always says you're quite funny sometimes. If people would only bother to listen to you.

50

But the point is that I'm not like them, you see. I could never be like her, turning out novel after novel, sometimes I think there's almost one a month, like the curse. And not like him, with all his . . . his sense of responsibility. Except . . . except the wanting-to-screw-around bit, I suppose. Yes, that could be Daddy's genes, all right. I saw them, you know. Him and that secretary who came down on the day of the accident – you and Mummy were at it in the garden – oh, I knew that didn't mean anything, it was all cuddles and comforts and tears and all that sort of stuff, grown-up, not sex. But when I went inside – there they were. *Really* at it. I could even see his erection. It was sticking up against his trousers. He looked sort of crazy. And now he's doing it with someone else, or possibly even someone else after the someone else, I hear him on the phone at night when he thinks we're asleep. Hear him creep down, then his voice – daddying away. Being responsible. What I don't understand is why I hate her for letting him get away with it and not him for doing it. But the truth is I do hate her, I hate her for everything, everything.

RONNIE: Why . . . why are you telling me all this?

NATALIE: Don't know. Wanted to tell someone who wouldn't gossip, and I expect you've taken vows of silence – anyway, you're not allowed to gossip about what your parishioners confess.

RONNIE: I don't think you qualify as a parishioner. (*Clearly upset.*) You've never once set foot in my church during service, not a single one of you. And it wasn't a confession. Which we don't hear anyway in the C.of E. It was sneaking, Natalie.

(NATALIE *looks at him in shock, runs to the bottom of the garden, in tears, sits down, obviously crying.*)

Oh God – (*Stands helplessly, looking towards her.*)

(LOUISE, *meanwhile, has clearly become stuck, has been walking about the sitting room, muttering to herself two sentences that we can't hear properly. As* NATALIE *runs off,*

*she makes a gesture of despair, turns, and strides through
into the kitchen.*

BEN, *hearing her coming, seizes newspaper, picks up empty
mug, pretends to be sipping from it, reading.*

LOUISE *enters kitchen, clearly having forgotten* BEN. *Pulls
herself up when she sees him.*)

LOUISE: Everything all right, Ben?

BEN: Oh yes, thank you, Louise, contentment itself. Just . . .
just enjoying this article. Fascinating piece. Fascinating.

LOUISE: (*Opening oven, taking out chickens, stabbing at them
pointlessly with a fork*) What's it about?

BEN: (*Looking desperately at page*) Oh, um – Law report.
Always enjoy them. Full of tit-bits of information. This
one's a claim for, um, damages. Arising out of
negligence. Some damned fool took his son fishing,
(*Skimming article, unaware of what he is reporting*) electric
cables, son's line caught, electrocuted, second, third
degree burns, suing Water Board for . . . for negligence.
(*Is now aware, stares in horror at page.*) I . . . um . . .
um . . .

LOUISE: (*Has banged chickens back in oven, hasn't listened to a
word*) How very interesting, I'm just going for a little
walk. I need to think – see you later. (*Goes out on to
porch.*

RONNIE, *meanwhile, has approached* NATALIE, *and stands
uncertainly, apologetically.*

BEN, *meanwhile, has made gestures of self-anger, banging
his head with his hand.*)

RONNIE: Natalie, my . . . my dear – I . . . I . . .

NATALIE: I'm sorry. I didn't mean to make you angry.

RONNIE: No, I'm sorry. My response was – utterly selfish.
Completely unpastoral. What's worse, unfriendly.
(LOUISE, *who has been about to hail* RONNIE, *checks
herself.*)

NATALIE: I don't see why you should have to be bothered –
(*Lights a cigarette.*)

RONNIE: Yes. I bloody well should be bothered. Simply

52

because I find it upsetting – but you've said so much I scarcely know where to . . . to . . . but I think probably the most important thing is what you said about your mother. I don't believe, whatever you think you feel, that you really do hate her.

NATALIE: Yes, I do. But don't worry. It's quite mutual. She thinks I'm shallow, boy-mad and selfish. All true. While I think she's . . . she's interfering and . . . and negligent and blinkered and just as selfish as me. More selfish. Because – (*Suddenly realizing*) it's stopped! (*Turns, sees* LOUISE.)

RONNIE: What? (*Looking around, sees* LOUISE.)

LOUISE: Ronnie! I didn't know you were here – why didn't you come in and announce yourself? (*Coming into garden, picking up cigarette butt of Natalie's as she passes swing.*)

RONNIE: Oh, I was just about to. But then Natalie and I found ourselves having a bit of a – bit of a gossip –

LOUISE: Natalie darling – I thought we had an agreement that if you *are* going to smoke in the garden you'd bring some sort of ashtray out with you –

NATALIE: Yes, sorry Mummy. (*Takes stub from her.*) I'll put it in the rubbish.

LOUISE: Thank you, darling.

(NATALIE *goes up the garden to the kitchen.*
RONNIE, *deeply embarrassed, as* LOUISE *watches him.*
BEN *starting to false life with mug and paper as* NATALIE *enters, then sees it's* NATALIE, *relaxes slightly.*)

BEN: Ah, hello there, Nat. What have you been up to?

NATALIE: (*Throwing butt into rubbish*) Just talking to Ronnie.

BEN: (*Excited*) Ronnie – he's here then! (*Getting up.*)

NATALIE: Yes. In the garden. Talking to Mummy.

BEN: Ah!

(NATALIE *goes on into sitting room, throws herself into a chair, and covers her face with her hands.*
BEN *stands uncertainly, yearningly.*)

LOUISE: (*With a painful smile*) So. Natalie's been filling you in on the family news, has she?

53

RONNIE: Yes, well – I don't expect she meant a word of it, really. Girls of her age – not that I know much about them but . . . but . . . I expect. You know. Hormonal (*Gestures*) changes.

LOUISE: That comes earlier, Ronnie. And later. At the moment Natalie's hormonally at her most harmonious.

RONNIE: Ah.

LOUISE: But she's perfectly right – I'm not patient with her. Not as patient as I should be. I do get irritated by her . . . her obsession with boys. I hear her on the telephone for hours, you know, and at all hours – and it doesn't sound like her at all. She puts on a different voice, manner – and so I probably say things I shouldn't, but then . . . but then – (*Stops*) she's also perfectly right about my being just as selfish and obsessed as she is.

RONNIE: Well, I expect it's hard, being a writer as well as a wife and mother –

LOUISE: I've just finished *The Daffodil Corner* by the way. Apart from two immensely difficult lines, that is. Did she tell you? I expect not.

RONNIE: No. Why, Louise, that's . . . that's . . .

LOUISE: It was prompted by you, you know, Ronnie. That story you told me – do you remember? How you were weeding around the daffodils over there (*Points in a different direction from Ronnie's hollyhock corner*) and how you thought you heard children – dead but in some odd way happy – sublimely happy, wasn't it? So that was the seed – it's a kind of ghost story, but more than that, I hope. Haylife and Forling's are going to put it up for the Booker prize.

RONNIE: Why, Louise, my dear – how . . . how . . .

LOUISE: Oh, it won't win, of course. And it wouldn't really mean anything even if it did. Except in terms of prestige and money. But what I'm really trying to say, Ronnie, is that – whatever the cost to other people as well as myself – I'd do it all again. Harden my heart if necessary, all over again. I couldn't have spent the last ten years any

54

other way. (*Looks at him.*) You think I'm wicked, don't you?

RONNIE: No, I – well, you know me well enough by now, Louise – wicked isn't a word that comes easily or often to my . . . my . . .

LOUISE: (*Puts her arms around him, hugs him*) No, I know. The soul of tolerance, that's my dear, dear Ronnie. And kindness.

RONNIE: Tolerance and kindness. (*Laughs hollowly.*) Yes, well, as I implied in my . . . in my . . . I'm no longer sure that those particular virtues have a soul – and if they haven't, what sort of soul does one have, if one has one at all – that's the question I still haven't answered yet, Lou. (*Looks at her pleadingly.*)

LOUISE: (*Slightly perplexed*) Oh, Ronnie, you're full of soul. Why, one only has to look at our garden to know that. It's never been so beautiful. You can see for yourself – absolutely full of soul. (*Laughs.*)

RONNIE: Yes, well actually that's Kevin Tomalin's soul you're looking at. You know, old Tomalin's nephew. He works in the slaughter-house at Chard. Oh, I suppose I should have mentioned in my . . . in my . . . he's always wanted to be a landscape gardener and when I asked him to keep an eye on it during those rather . . . rather . . . weeks when I had so much on my plate, sorting out her effects and arranging the funeral – and he's simply gone on doing it. I hope he'll let me have a go again eventually. I hope you and Harry didn't mind my writing to you like that. It occurred to me afterwards that you might have assumed it was just another of my – epistles from Great Yarcombe, keeping you abreast – and then when you opened it – the shock! But I needed someone to spill it out to, and you and Harry are the only . . . only – I hope you didn't mind too much?

LOUISE: (*Concealing incomprehension*) Not at all, Ronnie, we were both so moved . . . so moved. Harry was going to write back – we both were – and then thought we'd wait until we saw you – and could talk properly –

RONNIE: Thank you. I suppose I should have spared you some of my wilder . . . wilder thoughts at least. All that nonsense about the old pennies and the new 50p pieces – and of course the PS – almost as long as the letter, wasn't it? But – I had to make it absolutely clear, Lou. Did I? What did Harry think?

LOUISE: Well, he was a bit . . . a bit puzzled. And so was I, Ronnie. Really.

RONNIE: What I meant was . . . was – (*Lifts up his arms, stares up at the heavens, and shakes arms in desperate inquiry.*) and not . . . not . . . (*Shakes his fists in fury at the heavens.*

BEN, *who has made several tentative moves towards appearing on the porch, has gathered himself together, and surges on to it as* RONNIE *is in mid-shake.*

BEN *stands staring at* RONNIE.)

Hello, Ben – hello, old . . . old . . . I was just showing Wilemena – Louise, Louise – what one of our farmers does every morning when there's sunshine instead of rain – or the other way round. Depending on which there is, eh? (*Laughs.*)

BEN: Ah! Not their fault, Ronnie. They are what they are! Innocent devils. Like the rest of us. Innocent devils. And devilish innocents. Mustn't blame them. Threaten them with everlasting what's-it!

RONNIE: (*Stares at* BEN, *slightly perplexed*) Um? Yes, well, um, yes. That's true. Wouldn't want to do that, Ben. Under any circumstances.

LOUISE: Would you two excuse me for a – there's something I must finish before Harry and – I'll see you later.

(*Hurries off, up the porch, into the kitchen, and is almost about to go through into sitting room, when she remembers the chickens. She frowns in at them, begins to take them out, then pushes them back in, and goes towards sitting room.*

NATALIE, *alert to activity off in kitchen, snuffs out*

56

*cigarette in the toby jug, puts it on the mantelpiece, turns off*
*the television set, and hurries out of the door, right.)*

BEN: All a matter of understanding. Even types like old
Tomalin. Even the bull. Nobody had any choice. That's
the key and clue to the whole business, Ronnie. But you
know all that. In fact, you're the one who put me on to
it. Particularly keen to come down and say that to you at
last. Without you I'd never. No, never. Your words
came back to me at my hour of darkest need.

RONNIE: Well, I'm so glad – what words exactly, Ben?

BEN: Just after my Emily died. Told you all about it. That
first evening, before we bought the place, Harry and I.
You told me that God was looking after her. That she
was in Abraham's bosom. Asleep.

(LOUISE *has entered the sitting room, wrinkles her nose at*
*the smoke, and waves it away. Looks into toby jug, makes*
*an expression of disgust, puts it back on the mantelpiece,*
*then settles into chair. She takes out page in typewriter,*
*studies it, crumples it up, puts another one in, and begins to*
*type.)*

RONNIE: I said that, did I? Abraham's bosom? I must say it
doesn't sound quite . . . quite my . . .

BEN: All came back to me. Not only *your* words but bits and
pieces from across my life – a phrase here from
Singapore, a prayer in Chile – something my Emily said
to me one summer's leave in Gosport – and when little
Harry – three years old he must have been, asked me
about the sun coming up, why it bothered to come up
. . . oh, I'm not making great claims for myself, Ronnie,
no Pauline conversation, I know my place in the scheme
of things, you see. Just another little dot of a chap who's
had a . . . a tiny glimpse of the light, all very humble,
boring even, some might say. I mean, there I was,
skulking about in my little flat in Fulham, couldn't face
people, not even my own son because of what I'd done
to his son – spent hours – whole hours – day after day,
down on my knees, sobbing away. Wanted to give up

my life. Would have done. In a flash. But of course
nobody came and asked for it, did they? Well, what
could they do with it? Even worse that what I'd done
with it, for all I know. (*Laughs*.) So it gradually dawned
on me, all this penance and pleading and whining was a
lot of nonsense. Self-pity. And what was worse,
arrogant. Yes, arrogant. I . . . I, little Benjamin
Pertwee, take responsibility! The sheer effrontery of it!
Who am I to think I can take responsibility for his
decisions? Absolute bloody blasphemy, when you think
about it! Pardon my diplomatic language. (*Laughs*.) But
through all this I kept remembering what you'd said –
Emily asleep on Abraham's bosom. Do you see? (*Stares
at him intently*.) Emily. On Abraham's bosom. Yes.
That's when it hit me – slowly hit me, hit me very
slowly – bong, bong, bong. (*Thumps his head slowly but
powerfully*.) And except for you, Ronnie, without benefit
of clergy. Of course I went around to my local vicar,
decent enough little blighter in his way, but I could see
he didn't understand a word I was saying, behaved as if
I was inviting him for a round of golf or something, but
then he's got a drinking problem – anyway reeks of
alcohol – to hell with him, eh? – now I'm not saying
I've solved all the world's problems – not a bit of it.
What I do say is that if we take God's view then there
aren't any problems to solve. They're all his problems,
and he can solve them any way he wants to, as long as
we all end up on Abraham's bosom. There it is, in a
nutshell. Along with my thanks. That's what I came
down to say.

RONNIE: Well, thank you, Ben. Thank you for coming
down. But . . . but – look, I do think there's been a bit
of a . . . a misunderstanding here. You see, I don't
really think we can just shove all human responsibility –
*our* responsibility on to –

(BEN *lets out a kind of scream. He is staring at the gate,
through which* NIGEL *comes.*

58

NIGEL *is walking with a stick. His gored leg is in a calliper.*
*He is wearing dark glasses.*)

NIGEL: Ronnie – and Grandad! How good to see you at last.
Now I might get some decent fishing – I've missed it.
(*Limping over to* BEN, *puts an arm around him.*) And you
– (*Turning.*) Hello, Ronnie. Can't imagine coming back
to Little Paradise without finding you in the garden.
(BEN *stands, unable to speak, staring at him.*)

HARRY: (*Appears at gate, carrying a leg-strengthening
contraption, a mattress, a suitcase, other odds and ends, with
difficulty*) Hello, everyone. I wonder if someone can give
me a hand –

RONNIE: Yes, of course, of course. (*Goes to* HARRY, *takes leg
contraption, mattress.*) Here, I'll take these –

BEN: Here, let me! (*Hurries over, seizes contraption and
mattress from* RONNIE.)

RONNIE: No, I'm . . . I can . . .

BEN: I've got them, I've got them. (*Wrestling them away from*
RONNIE, *glances furtively at* NIGEL, *and almost runs up the
garden.*)

HARRY: (*Following*) Careful, Daddy – there's no rush, you
know. You coming in for a lie-down, Nigel?

NIGEL: Oh, no thanks, Daddy. Not yet anyway. A bit of
fresh air – perhaps a stroll with Ronnie.

HARRY: Right. I'll just go and tell Mummy we're here.

NIGEL: Would you mind a little stroll?

RONNIE: Love one.

NIGEL: Good. Just give me a minute to – (*Sits down, puts his
head back.*
BEN *entering sitting room, attempting to recover emotionally,
stares at* LOUISE.
LOUISE *rips sheet of paper out, puts another one in, turns,
looks at* BEN *almost blankly.*)

BEN: Harry and . . . and . . . they're . . . they're – where
shall I put these?

LOUISE: Oh, Nigel's room I should think.

BEN: What is this thing exactly? Can't quite make it out.

LOUISE: (*Impatiently*) Mmmm?

BEN: (*As* HARRY *enters*) This . . . this thing. What exactly – ?

HARRY: It's to help strengthen his leg muscles.

BEN: Ah. (*Looks at it in a kind of horror, as* HARRY *opens the door for him, right.*)

HARRY: Sure you can manage, Daddy?

BEN: Yes, yes – (*Struggles out.*)

HARRY: Hello, darling.

LOUISE: (*Finishing typing*) How's Nigel?

HARRY: A bit peaky from the journey. He's going for a little walk with Ronnie.

LOUISE: As long as Ronnie takes it easy –

HARRY: Oh, I'm sure he will, darling. But what have you been up to? Not changing anything, I hope. Haylife and Forling like it just as it is.

LOUISE: No, I've been struggling with a whole new creative experience. (*Smiles at him.*)

HARRY: You don't mean . . . you don't mean you've started another one already.

LOUISE: No, finishing *The Daffodil Corner*. With two sentences that have taken me hours and hours, and still didn't come to me until you were in the room. Here! (*Holding sheet out to him.*) The most important part of the book. Of my writing life, as a matter of fact. To me, anyway. I wanted to wait until I'd done something you wouldn't be ashamed to be named in.

HARRY: (*Reads out*) 'This book is dedicated to my Harry. Faithful to a fault.' (*Slight pause.*) Thank you, darling.

LOUISE: Don't you like it?

HARRY: Yes – it's lovely. Lovely.

LOUISE: There is something – what is it?

HARRY: Well, only that – well, perhaps 'my' Harry's a little . . . a little too – well, too 'between us'. I mean, something we don't really want to share with your public.

LOUISE: Oh. Yes, I see, it does sound rather . . . rather possessive. More for an infant son –

HARRY: Yes, or a dog even. Just 'To Harry' is fine, isn't it? And I wonder if – well –

LOUISE: What?

HARRY: Well, something else instead of 'faithful'. Um –

LOUISE: Why, what's wrong with it? Nobody could have been more supportive and loyal over the last seven novels –

HARRY: Yes, well those are the words, aren't they, darling? I mean faithful is used in such a . . . such a – limited sense, these days, it might be misinterpreted by, well, certain types.

LOUISE: Oh.

HARRY: I think that word you used – not loyal, the other one – 'supportive'. Who has been so 'supportive' – or 'for all his support'. Yes, that sounds really . . . really, doesn't it? 'To Harry. For all his support.' If you think I deserve it, of course. (*Kisses her.*)

LOUISE: Can I add – 'over the years'? 'To Harry. For all his support over the years.'

HARRY: Absolutely. And I have deserved it, haven't I? (*Kisses her again.*)

LOUISE: Oh, my darling, without you –

HARRY: Well, I'll just get these up to Nigel's room – and perhaps go and have a word with Daddy. I think he's a bit overcome. I've a feeling there's something, someone I've forgotten – what could it be? (*Makes for door.*)

LOUISE: (*Suddenly remembering*) Oh darling – Ronnie! Wilemena's dead.

HARRY: Oh, really! How?

LOUISE: Well, that's the awful thing. I've no idea. He told us all about it in one of his letters apparently – I hoped you'd read it. I think I just stuck it in your study without opening it, even.

HARRY: Oh. Yes, I think I did see it lying around – how embarrassing! Well, we'll just have to bluff our way through – it must be a relief for him, really.

LOUISE: Well, he was going on a bit about guilt, I suppose it

61

must have been, being Ronnie – and old pennies and
50ps and shaking his fist at someone – God, I suppose. I
couldn't really make it out –

HARRY: (*Affectionately*) Silly bugger! And now up to Daddy.
Talk about 'the narrow round. As on we toil from day to
day'. (*Grins at her, goes off, right.*)

LOUISE: 'To Harry. For his support – ' (*Sitting at typewriter*)
loving support. Love and support. Love and support
through the years. That's better. 'Love and support.'
(*Typing.*)

NIGEL: Right. Now let's give ourselves a whirl, eh, Ronnie?

RONNIE: Are you sure you're really up to – you really do
look a little . . . a little . . .

NIGEL: Well, I have to, actually. I'm getting pins and needles
in my good leg. But we'll keep ourselves confined.
Cabin'd, cribb'd and confined, eh? (*Rising with
difficulty*) I need a bit of support, I'm afraid.

RONNIE: Of course. How, um, how –

NIGEL: Let me do this. (*Puts an arm around Ronnie's
shoulder.*) And off we go.

RONNIE: (*After a pause, awkwardly*) Quite comfortable?

NIGEL: (*With a little laugh*) More comfortable than you, I
expect. (*They walk a few steps.*) Isn't it lucky that you
never did anything to regret in those days when you
used to take me church-visiting. No, don't stop –

RONNIE: (*After a long pause*) You knew then?

NIGEL: Well, you used to look at me with such sad eyes –
that there were times when I thought, oh well, if he
really wants to do whatever it is he wants to do, let him
do it. It probably won't hurt. But if I had let you you
probably wouldn't be able to hold me up now, when I
really need it, would you? From embarrassment, guilt –
the usual stuff.

RONNIE: It wasn't sexual, you know. Not really. Nothing
like it ever happened to me before. Or since. But I was
. . . was hopelessly in love with you. Loved you. And
sometimes the need to express it – somehow! I'd hate

you to think I'm just another Church of England vicar who . . . who gropes choir boys.

NIGEL: Don't be ridiculous, Ronnie – I've never thought of you as anything but the nicest man I've ever met. Of course, you could still be that and grope choir boys, couldn't you? But you'd never permit it. Forgive in others what you'd never permit in yourself is virtually your life's principle. (*Little pause as they walk.*) Look, I'm terribly sorry about your Mrs Mossop. I know how devoted you were to each other. It must be a dreadful loss.

RONNIE: Thank you.

NIGEL: I would have written back but –

RONNIE: But what? (*Little pause, then almost a cry.*) I longed for a letter from you!

NIGEL: Yes. I should have. Even – well, the truth is, Ronnie, I couldn't have written without telling you the truth.

RONNIE: And what would that have been? Something smart and Cambridge?

NIGEL: Well sort of. Tit for tat anyway.

RONNIE: Tit for tat?

NIGEL: Well, your tat was all that stuff about the awfulness of having only one 50p piece when you wanted to cover both her eyes, and that was the whole point of the old pennies, and how shocking it was you should have thoughts like that at a time like that.

RONNIE: I remember perfectly well – the point is those *were* my thoughts – my real thoughts – I mean, she was lying there in my kitchen, with a soup ladle in one hand, an onion in the other. She'd just keeled over while I was in the middle of one of my . . . my lectures on her attitude to an Irish Catholic family that's moved in –

NIGEL: (*Almost testily*) Yes, yes, I know. You described it all quite brilliantly – you made it perfectly clear that she'd died from boredom.

(RONNIE, *after a slight pause, laughs.*)

And then shaking your fist at God –

RONNIE: I didn't shake my fist! I didn't! If you'd read my PS
properly – I wagged my arms – my hands were a
question, not a . . . a threat. 'Why' merely, not 'How
dare you!' – like this – (*Shows* NIGEL.
NIGEL *laughs.* RONNIE *looks at him indignantly, then also
laughs.*)
You could have written back making fun of me. I
wouldn't have minded. I'd have been grateful. What did
you mean, tit for tat?

NIGEL: There's a simple thing you don't understand. That's
the tit.

RONNIE: About . . . about death?

NIGEL: Exactly.

RONNIE: (*Sarcastically*) And you understand it, do you?

NIGEL: Yes.

RONNIE: And what is it, pray tell, this . . . this . . . ?

NIGEL: Tit. Let me think how to put it. (*Pause.*) Yes. That
the living who – no. That's not it. That it's only the
dying who – no, (*Laughs*) that's not it, either. Oh well,
what it amounts to is that without death we wouldn't
know how to live.

RONNIE: And that's your . . . your . . .

NIGEL: Tit.

RONNIE: – and that old cliché! So why all this fuss and
bother and . . . and grief! Celebrate death instead
because it . . . it . . . thank you. I'm glad you didn't
write that to me! I'd have . . . I'd have . . .

NIGEL: I'm sorry, Ronnie, I was really only trying to find a
way of – well, communicating something rather
particular. Rather personal. To you. Without making
too much fuss and bother.

RONNIE: What do you mean? (*Still angrily, suddenly stops,
stares at* NIGEL.) It's not . . . not true!

NIGEL: I'm afraid it is. My head's getting worse and worse –
and I've always known – sensed – from when I was very
young – that it – had a purpose. An ultimate purpose.
To keep me alive to the thought of how close, how very

64

close I always am to death. And the thought of that has made all my other thoughts more real. I've loved that, Ronnie. I really have. The something wrong with my head, *in* my head, growing and growing to kill me, is what's made everything, *everything*, so valuable. (*Grins.*) I wish I'd had some sex, though. Proper sex, I mean. God, I'd have enjoyed it. I know I would. Especially with someone I loved. But apart from that one major regret, I'm grateful –

RONNIE: I don't want to know this! I don't want to know this! Why are you telling me this?

NIGEL: Well, because of Grandad, you see. They'll want to blame somebody, people always do, and he's the obvious candidate. He's already taken the rap for my leg. Although actually it was all my fault, I was much the older and more responsible party at the time. (*Little pause.*) Besides I'd have done anything to get out of going fishing. But the fact, the brute fact – according to chaps I've talked to at Cambridge and the books they've put me on to – is that the malignancy was in my brain from birth. A jolt anywhere, dancing, a tumble down the stairs when drunk – any accidental blow – could have set it off. Anyway, I'll make a deal. If I can tell them myself at the last minute I will. The master plan is not to give them a second's more grief than I have to. But I may miscalculate. As far as I can make out it could happen when I'm least prepared. Though I try to be always prepared. But it could be up to you, you see.

RONNIE: (*Almost to himself*) Now this – is intolerable. *This* is intolerable!

NIGEL: Oh, come on, Ronnie, think of the world – the horrors it sups on every minute of every day and every night. Children dying of starvation, children shot to death by other children or grown-ups even. And here I am, having had a wonderful life and having already exceeded the life expectancy of millions by years and years, loafing about in the midday sunshine of an

exceptional summer in an English garden. Here, in
Mummy's Little Paradise (*Gestures around it*) consulting
with a close friend and civilized soul (*Smiles*) on how
best to leave him and . . . and others I love – (*Sinks
during this into the swing*) so really to hell with me. And
Mrs Mossop even. We're the lucky ones. She went in
the middle of one of your sermons. I'll go full of . . . full
of (*Looks suddenly towards gate*) life. Hello.

NATALIE: (*Appears at gate*) Hi. Back then, are you? (*Coming
in.*)

NIGEL: Yup. Back.

NATALIE: (*To* RONNIE) She heard everything I said, didn't
she?

RONNIE: No, no, she – just a little bit of it, the last part of it.

NATALIE: That was the worst part. (*To* NIGEL) I said I hated
her.

NIGEL: Did you now? (*Laughs, over brightly.*) Well then, she
should know it. Do her no harm.

NATALIE: You all right?

NIGEL: Yes, yes, but I need to get in – lie down for a bit –

RONNIE: Oh. Well, can I . . . shall I . . . (*Puts his arm
around him.*)

NIGEL: No, Nat. Nat can do it. Can't you, Nat?

NATALIE: I suppose so. Come on then. (*Helps him up, gives
him her shoulder. They move slowly towards the porch.*
RONNIE *stands watching.*
NIGEL *mutters something in* NATALIE's *ear.* NATALIE
*giggles.* NIGEL *giggles with her. They go up the porch,
laboriously.*
HARRY, *during this, enters sitting room from right.*)

LOUISE: (*Hands him sheet*) Do you mind if I put in 'loving'
and 'devoted'? I can't bear not to express what I feel
about you in my own words. Rather than in yours, if
you see, darling.

HARRY: (*Looks down at page*) He's being a bit odd again.

LOUISE: Who?

HARRY: Daddy. When I went in he was lying there with

Nigel's leg contraption in his arms. He pretended to be asleep. But I'm sure he wasn't.

LOUISE: Oh. Well, I expect he's . . . he's upset. After all, it's the first time he's seen Nigel since – (*Gestures.*)

HARRY: That's true.

LOUISE: Tell me, what do you think? (*Indicating page.*)

HARRY: (*Looking down at page*) But there's something about him –

(NIGEL *and* NATALIE *have passed up the porch, through the kitchen, through the passage, and are now entering the sitting room.*)

LOUISE: Nigel darling – here you are then! (*Embraces him.*)

NIGEL: Ow! Sorry, Mummy, my leg's feeling a bit awkward. Need to lie down really.

LOUISE: Oh sorry, my love! But you look . . . look . . .

NIGEL: Fine, Mummy. Apart from my leg. All it needs is a rest.

HARRY: (*Putting page down on desk*) I'll see you upstairs. Help you to bed. (*Takes him around the shoulder, with paternal firmness and strength, and guides him through door.*)

NIGEL: (*As he goes*) Well, Nat can – Nat can manage –

HARRY: Not up the stairs she can't. (*Going out.*

LOUISE *looks at the page, then at* NATALIE.)

LOUISE: Darling, would you mind checking on the chickens and peeling the potatoes?

(NATALIE *makes to go.*)

And oh, darling, whatever your feelings about me – and I think I understand them – I wouldn't be a writer if I didn't, after all, (*Gives a little laugh*) do you think you could try not to share them with one of our closest friends?

NATALIE: Sorry. Didn't mean it. Didn't mean you to hear.

LOUISE: I know, darling, but we ought to think of Ronnie too. He's got quite enough to cope with – his poor wretched wife has just died, you see.

NATALIE: But he didn't tell me.

67

LOUISE: Well, darling, I don't expect you gave him the chance. Did you?

NATALIE: No. I'll do the potatoes then. (*Goes into kitchen.*

*LOUISE stares after NATALIE, suddenly stricken. Makes to go into the kitchen, hesitates, sits down at the table instead. Her eyes stray to the page. She picks it up idly, then examines it. Then begins to look at the pages of her typescript. Becomes involved, even laughing aloud, as she reads.*

*RONNIE, after Nigel's departure, has sat down on the swing, been swinging thoughtfully through the above. He begins to swing a little more vigorously, unconscious that he is doing so. Becomes involved in the swinging, higher and higher.*

*DRAYCOTT enters. He is carrying a flagon of cider. Stands watching RONNIE, who doesn't see him, then does.*)

RONNIE: (*Subsides*) Oh hello. I was just . . . just . . .

DRAYCOTT: Oh Christ! It's the homocidal vicar. (*He has clearly been drinking.*)

RONNIE: Sorry?

DRAYCOTT: We met years ago. Here. In this garden. And you assaulted me. Quite violently. I had to subdue you.

RONNIE: Did you really? Oh, of course I remember – well. Um, nice to see you again.

(*They shake hands.*)

DRAYCOTT: I had lunch with Harry yesterday. He invited me down – I wasn't sure whether he meant it, not even sure that I accepted, but here I am anyway. Question is whether I'll get anything to eat, eh? (*Sits down.*) Better not with my back to you. (*Turns to face RONNIE.*)

RONNIE: Why not?

DRAYCOTT: Well, when you came at me I had my back to you, seem to remember. Maybe something to do with the shape of my head. Or my neck. One of my girlfriends once said that I sometimes reminded her of a dog. Picked this up in the local. Pub. Had a few drinks. Stupid.

RONNIE: What was it about – our little – spat?

DRAYCOTT: I don't know. (*Opening cider.*) I expect I was in a bad mood. Stuck with my novel or something.

RONNIE: (*Suddenly remembering*) No, you'd just finished it! *Bugger Off.* Actually I kept an eye out for it – was it ever, um –

DRAYCOTT: Yes, yes, but not under that title. Harry made me change it. *The Rhubarb King* we decided to call it. (*Swigs from flagon.*)

RONNIE: Anyway, you're back with Harry then?

DRAYCOTT: I never left him. Didn't Harry tell you? (*Passes* RONNIE *the flagon.*)

RONNIE: No – actually he's never mentioned you from that day to this. I thought because of your – falling out. Actually, I often felt it was my fault. Felt quite guilty –

DRAYCOTT: That's Harry for you. Still, I couldn't possibly be with anyone else. He's like a . . . a . . . an older brother, really.

RONNIE: (*Swigs mightily from flagon, then has a look at the label*) Oh, it's the local brew. Better be careful. It's famously lethal.

DRAYCOTT: (*With interest*) Is it? I suppose it has to be to get through to the turnip-tops. (*Takes flagon, swigging more down.*)

RONNIE: What?

DRAYCOTT: The yokels. They probably need a heady brew.

RONNIE: Oh, they're not stupid enough to drink it themselves. They just sell it to the tourists. Their own tipple is vodka and lemon.

(DRAYCOTT *laughs, passes flagon back.*)

(*Swigging*) I wish I could think of one thing – one damned thing – to celebrate. Oh, of course, Louise's latest. Yes, Louise's latest book. Going to be put up for that prize – the Booker. Have you read it?

DRAYCOTT: 'Fraid so. Saw the manuscript lying around Haylife and Forling's. Couldn't resist dipping into it. (*Shakes his head sadly.*)

69

RONNIE: It won't win the Booker then?

DRAYCOTT: Oh, no. It's not bad enough to win the Booker. Just like all her others, as a matter of fact. Perfectly decent, over-written, rather average – and full of the usual middle-class stuff – marriages, infidelity, children, even this – cottage in the country – comic vicar. With a couple of ghostly infants thrown in. For significance.

RONNIE: Really? What sort of comic vicar?

DRAYCOTT: She only gets them published because Harry did a kind of deal with Haylife and Forling with her first, *Roses Are* – whatever crappy colour roses are. Red. Yes. They took that to make sure they'd get something else Harry had control of. It was by me.

RONNIE: *Bugger Off. Bugger All*, I mean.

DRAYCOTT: *The Rhubarb King*.

RONNIE: Sorry, yes.

DRAYCOTT: But actually it was the one after that. Originally entitled *Fuck You*. Published as *Dogs in their Dignity*. That was the one Harry did the Louise deal on. *Dogs in their Dignity*. Not that I minded – it's just that Harry had such a reputation for integrity in those days. But people at Haylife and Forling blabbed of course. So he's become a bit of a joke. Peddling his wife's writings to compensate her for his infidelities. Which she doesn't even seem to know about. Or care about. Nobody knows which. Still a damned . . . a damned good agent in lots of ways.

(*During this they have been passing the flagon companionably back and forth.*)

RONNIE: But he did it from love – love of a sort – doesn't that have its own . . . own integrity?

DRAYCOTT: I suppose so. I've never loved anyone enough to know. God, I see what you mean. About this stuff.

RONNIE: Yes, it really is, isn't it? So you've never . . . never been attached –

DRAYCOTT: Not really. Too frightened. The moment I find myself worrying about a girl – you know, thinking

70

they've been run over because they're late stuff – that
sort of thing – I dump 'em. Also children. Bringing 'em
into the world – no right to do it to oneself.

RONNIE: But isn't that the price of all affection? Not just
human either. I mean dogs . . . dogs worry.

DRAYCOTT: Do they, poor sods? And God, does he worry?

RONNIE: Hope not. If he does it means he hasn't got a clue
about what he's up to, doesn't it?

DRAYCOTT: Just like the rest of us, eh? And if he doesn't
worry, does it mean that all shall be well, and all manner
of things shall be well?

RONNIE: Yes. Either that or . . . (*Thinks*) he's on drugs.

DRAYCOTT: Still, he doesn't need to have existed to justify
himself. Think of all the great art he's provoked by not
existing. As well as by existing. Even types like me –
sent to a Church of England primary school, don't
remember anything educational about it except for the
morning service, the 23rd psalm for instance, The
Lord's My Shepherd I'll not want, He maketh me down
to lie/ Through pastures green He leadeth me/ The quiet
waters by.

RONNIE: No, that's not the psalm, that's the hymn. (*Begins
to sing it.*)

DRAYCOTT: You're right.

RONNIE: Of course I'm right. I'm a professional. (*Continues
to sing.*

DRAYCOTT *joins in, remembering the words as he comes to
them.*

LOUISE, *meanwhile, has been sitting as if transfixed by a
thought. She suddenly gets up, dashes into the kitchen, and
stares at* NATALIE. NATALIE *stares back, frightened.*)

LOUISE: You're absolutely right, darling, absolutely right.
I've been a rotten mother and I . . . I . . . I – love –
(*Lets out a sob, puts her arms around* NATALIE.)

NATALIE: No, you haven't, Mummy, no, you haven't, no,
you haven't –
(*They stand embracing.* HARRY *enters, right. He stands for*

71

a moment, then goes over to the desk, picks up sheet of paper, and reads.)

HARRY: 'To Harry. For his love and . . . and . . . (*Stops, almost choking in self-disgust.*

BEN *enters. He is carrying Nigel's leg contraption. He stares at* HARRY, *sightlessly.*

HARRY *turns, sees him. They stare at each other.*)
Daddy . . . Daddy . . . what is it?

BEN: My fault, Nig.

HARRY: I'm Harry, Daddy.

BEN: Forgive me, will you? Oh, please forgive me, Nig!
(*Sinks to his knees, lets out a howl.*)

HARRY: I'm Harry, Daddy! (*Goes to him.*)

BEN: (*Flailing at himself, and accidentally at* HARRY, *with leg contraption*) I did it . . . I did it . . . all my fault. Oh God, forgive me, please forgive me – help me, God, little Ben, little Ben – didn't mean it, didn't mean it, Nig!

(NIGEL *enters, in underpants, a leg-brace. He stands at the door.* BEN, *as if sensing his presence, turns towards him. They look at each other.*)
Forgive him, Ben, little Ben, Harry!

(NIGEL *goes to him, kneels down laboriously, puts his arms around him.* BEN *collapses into him, sobbing.*

*Meanwhile, in the kitchen,* NATALIE *and* LOUISE *are clutching each other tightly, sobbing freely and almost happily.*

DRAYCOTT *and* RONNIE *continue singing to the end of the hymn, in low, drunken voices.*)


SCENE TWO

*A year later. Garden at twilight. House not visible, as in Act One, Scene One. Sound of birds. Otherwise silence.* RONNIE *enters, stands staring towards the house, then sits down on the stump seat.*

72

HARRY *appears at the gate. He is carrying a briefcase, and has a raincoat over his arm.*

RONNIE: (*Stares at him*) Good God! Harry!

HARRY: Hello, Ronnie – you look as if you're seeing a ghost. Are you?

RONNIE: No, no, I – it's just that I haven't been here for such a long time – not since that last dreadful afternoon when you were down . . .

HARRY: And had to rush Daddy back to London. About a year ago it must be, mustn't it?

RONNIE: About that, yes, and then this afternoon I happened to be cycling past the front and saw the 'For Sale' sign up –

HARRY: This afternoon. Really? We put the place on the market weeks ago. I'll give the agents hell – one of the things I've come down to do.

RONNIE: So . . . so you've decided to sell then, have you?

HARRY: Well, we never seem to get down here any more. We thought we'd look for somewhere nearer London – if we look for anywhere else at all.

RONNIE: Well that . . . that certainly makes sense. And Louise – is she . . . is she . . . (*Looking towards house.*)

HARRY: (*Puts his raincoat and briefcase down on stump*) No. She refused to come. She agrees we ought to sell, but says if we do she can't face seeing the place ever again. Of course, in her heart – (*Pulls on swing ropes.*) Well, this still seems pretty firm – hope whoever takes it has children. Garden's in good shape.

RONNIE: Yes, young Tomalin's awfully proud of it – he's given up butchery entirely, you know. Set up as a landscape gardener. Hope he'll be allowed to keep this up. I really believe he'd do it for next to nothing he loves it so much. Could you – well possibly you could mention it to the estate agents – he asked me to but I didn't think it was quite my . . . my . . .

HARRY: Of course you can mention it, Ronnie. With my blessing. Full blessing.

RONNIE: Oh. Well, thank you. And how is – (*Hesitates*) old Ben?

HARRY: Quite calm now really. Apart from the occasional lapse. A few Sundays back he raced the vicar to the pulpit. Suddenly took it into his head he'd give the sermon, you see. (*Little laugh.*) Apparently there was quite a tussle before they managed to drag him down. The vicar was quite affable and understanding but if it happens again – (*Thinks*) won't be. Actually he had a smell about him – of drink.

RONNIE: Really? Surely Ben scarcely ever drank –

HARRY: No, the vicar. I expect in due course he's heading for a home. Daddy, I mean. But I want him to have as much freedom – that one your wife – perhaps you'd give me the address before I go back?

RONNIE: Of course. And Natalie? How's she?

HARRY: In six months I'll be a grandfather. That's how she is.

RONNIE: Oh! Well, that's . . . that's . . .

HARRY: A complete waste. Though actually we don't see too much of her. She seems to feel that contact with us, even in the womb, might lead to it being contaminated in some way. Morally, I suppose she means. She sometimes phones Louise up but won't speak to me at all. I don't know what I've done – mainly be an English middle-class male, I think. She's against all that – against the father too, although that doesn't necessarily mean he's a middle-class English male. She refuses to tell Louise anything about him. She's living in a hostel until they give her a council flat. One-parent families get special deals, you see. I've had to sign a document swearing I won't allow her to live at home. But what's a small lie – if that's what she wants. (*Smiles at* RONNIE.)

RONNIE: But I'm sure she'll – in the end – (*Then quickly*) And Nigel, how's Nigel? (*Waits with terror.*)

HARRY: Yes, well, he's the main reason we haven't been

down – or been anywhere much recently. It turned out
his headaches had been getting worse and worse, you
see – tried to keep them from us – everybody. Until
one night at Cambridge they heard him screaming. And
got him to hospital. That's when it began – scans,
probes, test after test and eventually they found it – or
thought they had. A secondary in the brain and the
primary in his testicles. They were going to do various
operations – and if they failed chemotherapy, I suppose
– I don't suppose he'd have born that. His hair falling
out, too frail to think or live or – anyway, it just
went away.

RONNIE: (*Who has listened in fatalistic horror*) What . . . what
do you mean?

HARRY: The growth – whatever it was – as if he'd willed it
away, almost. First the thing in his testicles, then his
brain – it does happen from time to time apparently.
Not often, but enough not to cause a stir in medical
circles. Or religious circles probably, come to that.
Louise, however, Louise thinks it was a kind of miracle.
Because of some – pact she made.

RONNIE: A pact? Who with?

HARRY: Well, God, I assume. Isn't that usually who one
makes pacts with?

RONNIE: Well, not necessarily.

HARRY: (*Thinks, laughs*) Oh, I see. But we believe in the
devil even less than we believe in God, don't we? So a
pact with him would be even more worthless, wouldn't
it?

RONNIE: Nobody wrote to me!

HARRY: Mmm? What about?

RONNIE: Well – Nigel. You didn't write. Louise didn't write.
He didn't write.

HARRY: But what was there to write about? As you didn't
even know he was ill – and then he wasn't.

RONNIE: Yes, yes, of course – I do see. It's just that he and I
used to keep up a correspondence –

HARRY: Yes. Well, you know the young – he'll write to you one day from Harvard –

RONNIE: Harvard?

HARRY: He's planning to do a course in comparative theology. Got a very charming girlfriend, by the way. A postgraduate student. Doing a thesis on T.S. Eliot. To tell you the truth I'm . . . rather proud of him.

RONNIE: With good reason. Good reason.

HARRY: Oh, by the way, I told Ted Draycott I was coming down. He said if I saw you, to be sure to give you his . . . (*Gestures.*)

RONNIE: Draycott? Oh yes. Thank you. And mine . . . mine back. (*Abstracted.*) Though I hated his last.

HARRY: Bit of an effort, wasn't it? But still, it might win the Booker. But what about you, Ronnie?

RONNIE: Me?

HARRY: Yes, your news. Is there any? Or does the church clock still stand at – five past eight, isn't it? And still banqueting sumptuously off good Mrs Glossop's dinners?

RONNIE: (*Stares at him*) Mossop.

HARRY: (*As if hearing something, slightly distracted*) What?

RONNIE: Mossop. Not Glossop. Her name. And it was lunches, not dinners.

HARRY: Ah. But cooking as well as ever, is she? Whatever meal by whatever name? (*Looking towards house.*)

RONNIE: As well as ever. Living as kindly as ever. As lovingly as ever. Here. In my – (*Pats heart*) As long as I live. Betty Mossop.

HARRY: Good that some things don't change, at least, eh? But, of course, so sorry about . . . about your wife – we never had a chance to talk, did we? (*Gets off swing, looks towards sitting room.*)

RONNIE: The fact is that while my poor, dear Betty is dead, Wilemena – her name is Wilemena – is in the best of physical health and is malevolence personified. Only the other day she phoned me up –

HARRY: (*Who has not been listening*) Ssssh! (*Listens.*) Can't you
    hear it?

RONNIE: Hear what?

HARRY: She's here. She must have come down on the train. I
    had a feeling she would. And she's at it again.

RONNIE: I can't hear anything.

HARRY: Oh God, I can't bear it! I just wanted a little peace.
    That's all I wanted. A little separation. A little –
    (*Gestures*) that was her pact. That she wouldn't – not for
    a while – that she'd take time off, just for a while. But I
    suppose the sight of the typewriter in its old place, (*Puts
    his hands to his face*) she couldn't resist –

RONNIE: But if . . . if the pact was with someone she doesn't
    believe in –

HARRY: A pact's a pact, it doesn't matter who it's with. If I
    do a deal with another agent, or a publisher, then that's
    it. That's a deal. Listen . . . listen to her . . . her rattle,
    rattle, rattle – rattling through my life – rattling my life
    away, our lives, all our lives, and do you know, at first I
    didn't want her to because I didn't think she'd be any
    good, and that she'd get hurt, and all the embarrassment
    for me, I knew I'd end up representing her, and then
    when I realized she did actually have a talent, a little
    talent, a little but definite talent, I began to encourage
    her, hoped it would take over, so that she'd stop
    worrying, worrying about me, worrying about the
    children – so that I could be free to get on with things
    that I wanted, needed – but God how I hated it really,
    hated it. Listen to it. It's a . . . a death rattle, that's
    what it is! It's killed Nat, it almost killed Nig –

RONNIE: But Nigel's well. Natalie's going to have a baby –

HARRY: – and killed my love. All the way down in the car I
    could hear it. I kept saying it to myself, only different,
    different – as I was coming down the stair, I met a self
    who wasn't there, he isn't there again today, I wish to God
    he'd run away – that's it, you see, that's it, that's what I
    am, somebody's husband, somebody's father, somebody's

son, somebody's agent, somebody's lover, but what I
keep asking myself is who are you? Who are you? (*Stares
at* RONNIE *uncomprehendingly.*)

RONNIE: Ronnie. I'm Ronnie.

HARRY: I've got to get free of it all, free of the . . . the . . .
rattle rattle rattle – I can't stand it – won't stand it . . .
it follows me everywhere – tell her that, tell her that,
Ronnie, would you please?

RONNIE: What, tell her . . . tell her that you're leaving her?

HARRY: (*Almost demented*) Yes, please, thank you, I'll go
back to London now – straight away – move out my
things – I'll live in the office until I can find somewhere
else, she can have the London house, she can have this,
I'll take it off the market if that's what she wants, I
know she still loves it, her . . . her . . . her little – and if
she wants to stay down here – yes, that would be best –
for her to stay down here. You could keep an eye on
her. You'd be wonderful companions for each other, and
. . . and if she goes on, keeping at it, I'll go on
representing her, promise her, much better for her, for
everyone, to have an agent who isn't her husband!
(*Stares at* RONNIE *in a kind of mad hope.*)

RONNIE: And you think I'm going to tell her that – all that?

HARRY: Why not? It's a . . . a pastoral duty.

RONNIE: What, to go breaking the news to wives that their
husbands are leaving them, the terms of the settlement –
you're not serious. You can't be, Harry!

HARRY: Why not? All I'm asking you to do as a man of God
is to lessen the hurt for somebody you claim to care
about. Why, I thought hurt-lessening was virtually all
you believed in. The sum total of your faith. Two
thousand years of Christian suffering – the virgin birth,
the crucifixion, martyrdoms, crusades, inquisitions, and
here . . . here . . . the climax of all that, the . . . the
complete spiritual *climax* of blood letting, suffering,
death – a little English chap who believes we shouldn't
hurt people if we can help it. Or don't you believe even

78

that much, Ronnie? Not enough to act on it –

RONNIE: (*Who has been standing trembling with rage through this, hurls himself furiously on* HARRY, *crying out*) How dare you! How dare you!
(*They tussle fiercely for a moment, then* HARRY *gets the upper hand, holds a still violent* RONNIE.)

HARRY: (*Releases* RONNIE, *raises his hands in surrender, backs away*) Sorry, Ronnie. Sorry. I don't know what . . . what got into me, really. I didn't expect to hear it, you see. Not down here. Ever again. Sorry. Sorry.

RONNIE: You're not really . . . not really . . . just going to walk out then?

HARRY: It's stopped!

RONNIE: What?

HARRY: Can't you hear it? The rattle? It's stopped. Look . . . look, I don't know what I'm going to do, but – if you could just talk to her for a while – about anything you like, but don't let her know I've arrived, eh? And I'll . . . I'll just go and sit in the car and sort myself out, or . . . or go down to London and – or – I don't know – but I can't see her – just a little time at least. (*Going to gate, opening it.*) Will you do that for me? One little lie? That's all. (RONNIE *nods.*) Thanks, Ronnie. And sorry. And . . . and . . . well, God bless! (*Touches him quickly on the shoulder, goes out, leaving gate open.*
RONNIE *stares after him, then closes the gate as* LOUISE *appears on the porch, clutching sheets of paper. He thus looks as if he's entering.*)

LOUISE: Oh, hello, Ronnie! I heard the gate – I thought it must be Harry – sometimes I hear it even when I can't possibly, but I was right, wasn't I, even if you're the wrong person. (*Laughs, her joyfulness evident.*) I don't mean the wrong person, just –

RONNIE: Not the right person. (*Smiles falsely.*)

LOUISE: You're *always* the right person, dear, dear Ronnie! But how did you know I was here? Not even Harry knows – I told him I wouldn't come down with him –

not if we were going to sell. I told him I'd never set foot
down here again –

RONNIE: Well, actually, I saw the 'For Sale' sign outside,
and couldn't resist popping in for a look – old times –

LOUISE: Isn't it beautiful! (*Looking around.*) And the garden
– thank you, my dear, kind, best Ronnie. (*Kisses him.*)

RONNIE: Actually, young Tomalin – I was just saying (*Stops
himself*) to myself –

LOUISE: We can't, you see! We simply can't!

RONNIE: What?

LOUISE: Sell! I won't let us. I knew I couldn't let him! The
moment I came in – I'd been so frightened on the train
that I wouldn't even recognize it any more after such a
year – such a dreadful, dreadful year – and the moment
I came in and saw – things, my typewriter, just as I left
them, just as they always were when I came back – I was
always the first through the door, you know – and look,
just look, how is it the sun always shines here? No, I
can't let it go, we won't let it go. This is where I wrote
*Roses Are White*, this is where I wrote *The Daffodil
Corner*, this is my past, mine and Harry's, Natalie's and
Nigel's, and whatever's gone wrong for a while, you still
can't, you haven't the right to just shove it aside, our
past, and put a 'For Sale' sign on it. So . . . so, I have
written my poor darling a letter. A begging letter – can I
read it to you? Or would I be keeping you from your
beloved Mrs Mossop and one of your sermons and her
dinners? (*Laughs.*)

RONNIE: She . . . she only does my lunches, Louise. But do
you think – a private letter – and to Harry – that I really
ought – ?

LOUISE: Oh please, Ronnie! You've been such a part of
everything that's happened here, and if I strike a false
note –

RONNIE: (*After a little pause*) It would be a great privilege,
Lou. Thank you very much. (*As* LOUISE *goes to sit on the
swing, he goes to the stump, picks up Harry's briefcase and*

raincoat, realizes their significance, puts them down again hurriedly, and sits down on top of them. He therefore has a slightly lop-sided and uncomfortable look.) Um, fire away.

(LOUISE looks at him, slightly surprised.)

RONNIE: I mean – (Gestures.)

(LOUISE smiles radiantly, then looks down.)

LOUISE: My darling Harry. My darling, darling Harry. How much easier it is to talk to you in my head when you're not here. I've got into the habit over the years of saying all the things I really want to say to you when you're not here to say them to, so this is a love letter, my love, that comes out of all the dark times we've been through together. It's also, my love, a begging letter. As I sit here writing it, my ear is cocked for you, a dog's ear cocked for the click of you at the gate and then your tread up the garden. And if you're not here by the time I have finished I shall go out and wait for you, and there will be the swing as it's always been since the children were – well, children – and there will be the stump that was your very personal enemy. An affront to your manhood. (Laughs, looks at RONNIE. RONNIE laughs back.) Until you subdued it by making it your friend and servant. The most comfortable seat in Devon. (Looks at RONNIE again, who strives to look comfortable.) Everything will be as it always has been and all my memories of all our summers will join up into one summer, with all the dark spots gone. And all the summers still to come already joining up in memory and anticipation – oh, Harry, darling Harry – (Stops, unable to go on because she is crying; it is not clear whether from happiness or grief, no longer reading.) Why have we been away from each other for so long! Why have we? (Stares, weeping at RONNIE.

RONNIE tentatively makes to get up, remembers what he's sitting on, sits down again.)

*Faber Drama*

W. H. AUDEN
ALAN AYCKBOURN
PETER BARNES
SAMUEL BECKETT
ALAN BENNETT
STEVEN BERKOFF
ALAN BLEASDALE
ANNE DEVLIN
T. S. ELIOT
BRIAN FRIEL
ATHOL FUGARD
TREVOR GRIFFITHS
CHRISTOPHER HAMPTON
DAVID HARE
TONY HARRISON
VÁCLAV HAVEL
SHARMAN MACDONALD
FRANK McGUINNESS
RICHARD NELSON
JOHN OSBORNE
HAROLD PINTER
DENNIS POTTER
SAM SHEPARD
TOM STOPPARD
TIMBERLAKE WERTENBAKER
NIGEL WILLIAMS